D1739757

HALF WILD

RHYANNON BYRD

MADISON HAYES

ELLORA'S CAVE
ROMANTICA PUBLISHING

An Ellora's Cave Romantica Publication

www.ellorascave.com

Half Wild

ISBN 9781419963421
ALL RIGHTS RESERVED.
Half Wild Copyright © 2008 Madison Hayes & Rhyannon Byrd
Edited by Pamela Campbell.
Cover art by Syneca.

Electronic book publication June 2008
Trade paperback publication 2010

This book is a work of fiction and any resemblance to persons, living or dead, or places, events or locales is purely coincidental. The characters are productions of the author's imagination and used fictitiously.

HALF WILD

Dedication

ဆာ

This book is dedicated, with a great deal of affection, to all the wonderful readers at our Pure Magick newsletter group! Thanks so much for sticking with us, you guys, and for enjoying our boys. *g* We look forward to watching the group grow...and can't wait to take you all along for the ride!

New members can find us at
http://groups.yahoo.com/group/PureMagick

Trademarks Acknowledgement

ဆာ

The author acknowledges the trademarked status and trademark owners of the following wordmarks mentioned in this work of fiction:

Barbie: Mattel, Inc.

Cubs: Chicago National League Ball Club, Inc.

Doc Marten: Dr. Martens International Trade GmbH Corp.

Hummer: General Motors Corp.

White Sox: Chicago White Sox, Ltd.

Chapter One
Guys Like That

ഔ

Sam's eyes followed the blond male model, her pure green gaze firmly snagged on his tight butt as he sauntered past. His cocky swagger announced to everyone within sight that he knew *exactly* how fine his rear view looked.

"I saw that," Jerri accused in a low whisper from the opposite side of their booth, her raised brows disappearing beneath the fringe of her bangs.

"Yeah," Sam murmured without adjusting her gaze. "I saw that too."

Jerri laughed, pulling her thick black hair over one shoulder. "That's not what I meant and you know it. I caught you checking out that model's ass…sets," she finished carefully as an older couple strolled past their booth.

Sam gave her a curt nod. Her chin length brown hair bounced lightly to frame her round face. "And the man's *ass*ets were firmly in place." She sighed, sounding wistful. "Wish we could afford a model like that for our stall. Bet we'd sell these dusters like hotcakes."

"Beefcakes," Jerri giggled as she corrected her.

Sam turned to her friend and grinned. "Good one," she acknowledged as a slender blonde slowed outside their booth, her eyes resting on a red vinyl duster. Tilting her head in interest, the woman moved into the booth, toward the rack of coats.

Soft brown eyes still flashing with humor, Jerri moved to assist their first customer of the morning.

It was the second day of the weeklong Annual Clothing Convention at Janus Palace in New Las Vegas. The two friends' clothing booth featured remakes of vintage clothing from the turn of the century. Blue jeans were making a strong comeback in the year 2050 and long black dusters were especially popular. In business only two years, Jerri and Sam had decided to attend the clothing convention in the hopes of attracting overseas orders. All the big international buyers were expected to attend.

So far, they'd sold three dusters to individual shoppers and had orders for a grand total of five more. It was hardly the auspicious beginning they had hoped for.

"Maybe I'll think about it and come back," the slender blonde told Jerri, using the same phrase they'd heard at least a dozen times so far.

"That would be great!" Jerri bubbled enthusiastically while Sam's expression turned wry.

"Maybe I'll think about it," Sam mimicked snidely as the woman tottered away on her tall spiked heels. "She'd better start thinking today if she hopes to make any sort of decision by the end of next year."

"Don't be mean," Jerri chastised her friend. "You're just jealous because she's thin and you're..."

"Not," Sam finished flatly. "And she wasn't thin. She was a freaking toothpick."

Jerri snuffled another soft giggle and put the vinyl duster back on its hanger.

"Here comes another one," Sam reported as a second model strode past, this time a dark man with shoulder length brown hair that looked softer than the mink coats being sold around the corner from their booth. "Yup," Sam sighed. "That's what we need, all right."

"I agree," Jerri said, trailing her fingertips down the slick surface of the duster's sleeve. "But if I could afford a man like that, I'd do more than put a coat on him," she taunted her best friend.

"Yeah?" Sam drawled. "And what exactly would you put on him, Ms. Burton?"

Jerri gave her a mischievous grin in answer.

"Does it begin with the letter…'C'?" Sam teased. "And can you put it on with your mouth?"

Feigning shock and disgust, Jerri made a face at her best friend.

Sam sighed again. "Maybe if we pooled our resources, we could afford a night—"

"Hey! I was just kidding," Jerri cut in. "I'm not paying a guy for sex, so don't go getting your hopes up. *I'm* holding out for true love," she added dramatically…and laughingly.

"Good," Sam nodded, blowing a wayward strand of deep honey colored hair out of her eyes. "You do that. But let me tell you, Jerri. True love for us *ain't* gonna look like that!"

"Speak for yourself, Hayward," Jerri growled in response. "I've dated nice-looking men before."

Sam rolled her eyes and made a soft, snorting sound. "Nice looking, yeah." She tilted her head toward the model's departing backside. "But guys like *that* don't just fall out of the sky."

Those words were followed by a large, jolting crack of sound and a brief flash of blinding light. Blinking against the dark spots that swam before her eyes, Sam grabbed Jerri's arm as they stared at a point just outside their stall where curling wisps of blue smoke wound up through the air along with the biting scent of burnt ozone. Together they watched the fragile drifting strings of vapor as the strange phenomenon slowly cleared to reveal two tall, naked men crouched in the middle of the convention center.

As the men straightened their long, hard limbs, they glanced warily about, their keen eyes narrowing as they took in their surroundings.

"They're...twins!" Sam goggled with surprise while Jerri nodded silently at her side.

"Not only that," Jerri rasped hoarsely, "but they're freaking gorgeous twins."

Together they gaped at the two male beauties. Both men were several inches over six feet tall with straight black hair and dark tans. The hard planes of their facial features curved into strong square jaws and wide curving mouths, while piercingly blue eyes swept the convention center. Although they wore no clothing, it would have been a mistake to say the men were completely naked. Each of them sported a silver mask which covered the upper half of one side of his face. While one of the men wore the mask on the right side of his face, the other twin's mask covered the left side of his rugged features.

Jerri's mouth dropped slowly open as Sam swallowed hard.

"Jerri," Sam mentioned sensibly in nothing more than a pale whisper, "those men look like they could use some coats."

Grabbing two long black dusters from their hangers, Jerri shoved one of them into Sam's hands. "Okay," she told her friend, "but I get the one on the left."

"Are you mad?" her friend muttered from the side of her mouth. "They're identical."

"You're not looking where I'm looking," Jerri argued with a tight laugh as Sam's eyes dropped from the men's faces down to their groins. Briefly her eyes shuttered from left to right. "Oh my god," she croaked. "Good point."

"Yeah, it is," Jerri answered, unable to rip her gaze away from such startling male perfection. "And like I said, it's all mine."

At that instant the man on the right turned slightly as his gaze found Sam's face. At the same time his cock gave a slow, lazy stretch, like something surging to life before their very eyes. Again, Sam's gaze shuttered, watching the man's thick, fleshy length spurt ahead of his twin's. "I...I can live with that," Sam replied thickly, taking an eager step forward.

Wondering if they looked as awed as they felt, the two women approached the dark, beautiful men, dusters in hand, doing their very best to keep their eyes above the long, thick erections now bobbing so beautifully before those magnificent bods. They resisted staring at those mouthwatering male organs — more from a sense of self-preservation than forced politeness. Of course, when their gazes — one green, one brown, both burning with avid sexual interest — dropped south a time or two in the brief moment it took to reach the men, they figured that self-preservation was about to take a gloriously extravagant leap out the nearest window.

With a warm smile on her lips, Jerri held out the duster to the twin on the left, his deep blue eyes glittering with intense interest as he looked her over. "Here, you can put this on." She eyed his broad shoulders with warm, female appreciation. "It *should* fit."

Sam handed her duster to the other one, and after exchanging a speaking glance, the two warrior-sized men slipped their arms into the long black coats then looked expectantly back at the women.

Sam frowned as she realized that several conventioneers, all of the female variety, had stopped near the tall pair, their eyes wide and mouths all but gaping at the sight of the gorgeous duo. It was on the tip of her sharp tongue to tell the poachers to scram when the man before her grabbed her arm and pulled her so close that she had to tilt her head back in order to stare up into those brilliant blue eyes. "What's the date?" he asked in a low, husky voice, dragging his hot gaze over her face, the short cut of her hair, then looking pointedly at her breasts.

"Um..." she hummed, feeling her wits scatter beneath the intensity of that searing appraisal. Shaking her head in bemusement at her schoolgirl reaction to an attractive man, she finally managed to mumble, "Er…it's July twenty-third."

"What year?" he demanded as his gaze moved to her mouth and stayed for a long, meaningful study that quickly had her softly panting, while her palms went embarrassingly damp and her earlobes thrummed with heat.

She only hesitated a second, wetting her lips with the tip of her tongue, before answering. "Two thousand fifty."

The grip of his fingers tightened for a moment and then he turned to the twin standing with Jerri. "It worked," he told his companion.

"What worked?" Sam asked, at the same time Jerri quickly said, "Okay, first things first. We, um, need to get them out of here."

Sam nodded her agreement, ready to get the studs away from the dreamy-eyed women beginning to collect around them, when the man standing with Jerri said, "Where is here?"

"You don't know where you are?" Jerri asked, her soft brown gaze wide with surprise, cheeks flushed with vibrant color against the dark fall of her hair.

"If I did, would I have asked?" he replied, his wide mouth twitching with humor as he arched one dark brow.

Sam sighed, shooting a telling look at Jerri. "Why do all the gorgeous ones have to be smart-asses?"

The one still holding her arm laughed softly beneath his breath. "She called you an ass, Deuce. I think mine's got some brains."

Ignoring the taunting comment, Deuce said, "We were trying for Jane-us Palace. This is the Palace, isn't it? All we've ever seen are the floor plans."

"Janus Palace," Sam corrected him. "Jaaanus."

He gave her an impatient frown. "No need to baa at me. I'm not a farm animal."

The man holding Sam's arm bristled. "Evidently the pronunciation has changed over time," he stated defensively.

"Possibly with good reason," his twin returned snidely.

"What do you mean?" Sam queried, shaking her head. "Mr. Janus —"

"Turns out to be a bit of an ass," Deuce finished for her.

His companion argued almost immediately. "Jane-us got a bum rap."

"Well I hope someone raped his ass, Four. Because he more than deserved it."

"Four?" Sam blurted out. "Your name is Four?"

He turned and gave Sam a sharp, penetrating stare. "My name is Kar'four but Four will do. This is my brother, Kar'two."

"Deuce," his twin corrected him.

Kar'four's gaze deepened as it roved down her body again, before slowly returning to her eyes. "You're women, aren't you? Real ones."

Sam tried to stifle her surprised snort. "These two are really quick," she muttered from the side of her mouth.

Jerri jabbed her in the ribs as she continued to smile determinedly up at Deuce. "I wasn't going for brains when I picked mine," she warned tightly. "I'm Jerri," she said, nodding encouragingly as she introduced herself. "And this is my friend, Sam."

Kar'four continued to stare down at Sam. "They're women, Deuce."

Without actually removing his eyes from Jerri's face, the one named Deuce cut his companion a condescending smile. "I got *that* part figured out, Four. But what's amazing is that they look like *real* women."

Four snorted. "And what do you know of what real women look like?"

Deuce's smile flashed wider, wicked and white within the deep tan of his face. "There's no way in hell breasts like *those* could be fake," he laughed gruffly, dropping his gaze to Jerri's firm mounds, her nipples pressing against the thin fabric of her shirt in sharp little points that seemed to demand his immediate attention.

"Yeah, *real* breasts," Four rasped, his voice sounding a bit huskier than before. "I never imagined they could look like *that*, though," he added, staring hungrily at Sam's abundant chest.

Deuce snorted. "You knew they'd be better on a real woman."

"Yes but I didn't expect them to be so different from the Synnies."

"Before I ask what the hell a Synnie is," Sam mumbled, cutting their strange conversation short as she took Four's hand and began dragging him along behind her, "we need to get you two outta here, just like Jerri said. You're attracting too much attention," she muttered, glaring at the same leggy blonde in spiked heels who had just been in their stall. The woman had stopped a few feet away, her big blue eyes burning with sexual interest at the two duster-clothed males.

Jerri grabbed Deuce's hand and pulled him along after Sam and Four. She expected to see his mouth hanging open with rampant lust as they passed the blonde beauty queen but when she turned, his expression was clearly dispassionate. Strangely, he didn't even seem to notice the woman.

They reached the long row of opulent elevators and quickly pulled the men into an opening door, then Sam hit the close button before anyone else could enter. They had a long ride ahead of them, since their rooms were on the 160th floor and the elevator traveled at a leisurely pace, the high definition screens on the insides of the doors regaling them with a steady stream of suggestions as to how they should spend their money in New Las Vegas.

Studying the dark beauty standing at her side, Jerri's eyes lingered on his mysterious silver mask, then flicked to the wide curve of his mouth for a brief moment before settling back on his warm gaze. "You didn't even spare a glance for the blonde back there. Didn't you think she was beautiful?" she questioned.

His mouth twisted. "She looks like a Synnie. I bet she even squeaks."

"What exactly does a Synnie look like?" she asked, wondering if that was the name applied to women from their country...wherever their country was. They clearly weren't from around there.

And she wasn't even touching the "squeaking" comment. *Ick*.

"Tall, blonde, reed thin with bright white teeth and plastic faces." He sighed, seeming bored with the idea.

Both women laughed softly. "Well," Jerri said, smiling wryly, "no one can accuse *us* of looking like Barbie dolls."

"Women," the man beside Sam said. "You look like *women*." The word seemed to roll off his tongue like a sumptuous treat, something meant to be savored slowly and sweetly with thorough satisfaction. "Like something out of a Titian or a Botticelli."

Sam arched her brow at his knowledge of the old masters but before she could comment, Deuce lowered his face to the curve of Jerri's throat and sniffed loudly, murmuring, "And you don't smell."

His voice came in a low, rough rumble of sound that stroked down Jerri's spine like a sweet, meandering drop of warm oil, while Sam snickered softly.

The pure evocative huskiness of that male voice, with its odd cadence, made Jerri feel sticky and warm, her cheeks flushed while something down deep inside her seemed to melt and ease. It was a strange, somehow new feeling of discovery, of awakening, though she was hardly a virgin. No, she'd known men but then something told her that she'd never known anyone like this magnificent male standing before her. He was, quite simply, out of this world. "Um...it's nice of you to notice. But what is it exactly that I don't smell like?"

"Like our women," he muttered, still rubbing his nose beneath her ear, breathing in long, deep breaths of her. "Like a Synnie."

Her nose scrunched as she shot a wondering look at Sam, who stared at the two of them with a small grin curving her wide mouth. "I should be afraid to ask, but exactly what do your women smell like?"

"'Cross between latex and hydraulic fluid."

"Ew." She laughed, while Sam murmured, "Charming."

"You're softer too," Four rasped, lifting his hand to rub the back of his knuckles across the curve of Sam's cheekbone, then trailing his dark hand over her jaw, down the white line of her throat. "Softer than the priceless silks of Pantrark."

"Yeah." Deuce laughed softly, a low, provocative breath of sound that stroked against the fluttering pulse at the base of Jerri's throat. "I bet they don't even squeak when you ride them."

"Oh honestly," Sam snickered, her cheeks flushed with color as Kar'four continued his provocative stroking along the smooth ridge of her collarbone, skimming inside the collar of her shirt to investigate the purely feminine curve of her shoulder. "What do you guys date? Robots?"

"Synthetics," they said in perfect unison.

Sam rolled her eyes. "I knew I shouldn't have asked. I should learn to keep my mouth shut."

A hot smile softened the hard slash of Deuce's mouth. "We've no women in our time. Only synthetic replicas— Synnies—and they're meant purely for sexual function."

Jerri's mouth fell open in shock, while Sam's green eyes went narrow with skepticism. "And what exactly is *your* time?"

"Twenty-two fifty."

"*Right,*" Sam drawled, obviously not believing them and the two men laughed, not the least bothered by her sarcasm. Oddly, they rather seemed to enjoy it.

Jerri's head cocked to the side as she studied the two identical beauties, her burnished gaze wandering several times to the metallic masks covering opposite sides of their ruggedly attractive faces. The rich silver metal appeared to be flexible, flowing and reshaping itself against their faces with every change in expression. "Sam, why can't they be from the future?" she argued.

"Because last I heard, Jerri," Sam muttered, "time travel still wasn't a part of our reality."

"Yeah but then naked studs falling out of the sky wasn't necessarily on our daily menu either," Jerri pointed out with a streak of stubbornness.

Sam's head nodded in thought. "Point taken." She stared at Kar'four for a long, heavy moment, then sighed and said, "So in this so-called future that you're from, what else don't your women do?"

"They don't talk as much, that's for sure," Deuce said dryly, pulling away from the tender spot he'd been nibbling beneath Jerri's ear, to glare a frustrated look at Sam.

Kar'four blew out an impatient snort at the other man's complaining, while his dark gaze held a speculative gleam as he studied Sam's lush body, lingering over the heavy swell of her breasts, the full curve of her hips. Very softly, he said, "They don't come, either."

"Oh," Sam whispered, tugging at her collar, feeling the temperature spike with every second that went by as that hungry blue gaze seemed to devour her, eating her up. For some unfathomable, wonderful reason, the mysterious stranger named Four didn't seem to care that she wasn't what society considered the perfect shape or figure or whatever they wanted to call their so-called feminine ideal.

But the way this man looked at her made her feel like a siren—like a woman capable of…of…whatever she set her damn mind to.

"I've a need to know what it feels like," he went on to explain, his voice a rich, husky rasp as he moved forward and pressed her into the mirrored surface of the wall at her back. "To have a woman—a *real* woman—go all soft and liquid on me, around me, clenching like a throat." His mouth twisted with a wry expression. "Only, I've never felt *that* either. I've read about it in ancient journals that record the way things used to be but I've never *felt* it."

She swallowed thickly. "If you're really from when you say you are, then why are you here?"

"We have our reasons," he responded, his dark gaze snagging, then capturing and holding her now hazy green one. "We'll explain them eventually, but there's something I *want* first. Something I *need*."

"What?" she demanded breathlessly, wondering when her voice had become that airy whisper of sound.

He stared straight into her eyes, deep, rich blue penetrating soft green and in a husky tone, he said, "I want to feel you come, *Sam*. I want to feel it *now*."

She gasped a soft, shaken sound of surprise…and he reached for the button on her jeans.

Chapter Two
We Can Explain Everything

അ

As Four reached for the button that snugged Sam's vintage jeans around her hips, she snatched at his hands. Her trembling fingers tangled with his as she fought for possession of the shining bit of brass that barred entrance to her pants.

"Kar'four," she squealed, somehow managing to sound forceful and turned on all at the same time. "You can't just...you don't just..."

Ignoring her protests, Four continued his attempt to wrestle his way into her pants. Without warning, he grasped her wrists and planted them beside her face, against the mirror at her back. Holding her against the elevator wall with the long press of his hard, duster-clad body, he looked down on her through narrow blue slits that smoldered with purely sexual intent. "Why not?" he demanded in a low rasp.

Like a deer caught in a car's headlights, Sam stared up into his brilliant blue gaze. "Why not?" she mouthed faintly.

"Yeah," Jerri prompted her after a moment of empty silence, "Why not, Sam?"

"I. Um. Give me a minute," Sam answered weakly, "I'm sure I'll come up with something...eventually."

Deuce snorted. "I could come up with something right now," he intoned dryly.

"And *I'm* way ahead of you," Four breathed out in a competitive murmur.

Jerri giggled, taking mercy on her friend. "I think Sam's trying to tell you guys that public displays of sex aren't exactly tolerated in our time," she offered helpfully.

"Yeah," Sam said distantly, nodding her head until a dark, honey-brown lock of hair curled over her left eye. "Yeah. That would be it."

Lifting one dark eyebrow, Four cut a glance to either side of the elevator. "This place doesn't look very public to me," he growled in a dark, defensive rumble.

When he moved his hips slightly, Sam got a tantalizing taste of his thick erection pressed against her belly. At almost the same time, the elevator gave a light bounce and the doors opened on the 160th floor, where three couples waited to board the car.

"Now it does," Deuce drawled, snickering beneath his breath, clearly enjoying his twin's bad sense of timing.

Reluctantly, Four separated himself from Sam then followed Jerri and Deuce through the elevator doors, his fist still clamped around one of Sam's wrists.

Hurrying down the hall, Jerri waved a key at a door then pushed inside the hotel room.

Deuce sauntered in behind her, watched the door close behind Sam and Four, then smiled at Jerri. His expression was both smug and predatory. His unbuttoned duster fell open as he took two slow steps toward the blushing brunette. "So much for public places," he warned her in a low rasp. Jerri had only time enough to raise her hands between their bodies before he had her up against the wall. Immediately, he sucked in a harsh, strangled gasp. "Oh," he choked, "By my Ocean Mother. Don't stop doing that."

With her palms flat on the mouthwatering perfection of his muscle-sculpted chest, Jerri stopped pushing for the time being. "Don't stop what?"

"*That!*" he said in a low, husky murmur. "*That.* Don't stop…touching me. With your hands, woman."

Jerri frowned at her fingers splayed out on Deuce's broad chest. With a sneaky smile, she moved both palms a few experimental inches, stroking the firm, sleek skin beneath her touch.

"Mmm." Deuce closed his eyes and sighed. "Four. You've got to try this." He opened his eyes suddenly to gaze down at Jerri. "Do it again," he demanded.

With a deep, warm giggle, Jerri moved her hands fractionally.

Again Deuce closed his eyes, obviously enraptured.

Across the room, Sam was still wrestling with Kar'four. Catching the look on Deuce's face, Sam worked her hands inside Four's coat and gave him a solid push. "You can't just do this," Sam grated at him.

Her hands on Four's chest seemed to slow him somewhat. Frowning down on her, he pushed his chest against her hands, taking a moment to savor the new sensation before he spoke. "You said that before. But you didn't say *why*. The articles I read about female sexuality indicated that women liked sex as much as men."

"Oh yeah?" Sam gritted. "What were you reading, Einstein?"

"Ancient documents from…*Erotic Weekly*."

"Oh," she muttered, rolling her eyes. "Well that explains a lot."

His brows rose in surprise — one black, the other moving beneath the flow of metal that covered the right side of his face. "You've read them?"

Sam halted, chewing her bottom lip. "Do I look like the sort of woman who reads erotic fiction?" she finally asked Four.

"I've read a little," Jerri volunteered cheerfully.

"You would have," Sam complained darkly.

"You have too," Jerri protested, laughing.

"Only one or two stories," Sam said defensively. "Ten at the most," she finally admitted after a long pause. Turning her gaze back on the smirking male crowding into her, she said, "So you've read some erotica, Four. Good for you. Tell me— during your extensive studies, did you happen to pick up on anything about relationships... feelings...courtship?"

Four frowned thoughtfully. "Are you talking about foreplay?"

Jerri laughed outright, making the corner of Deuce's mouth kick up into a satisfied grin.

"That would do for starters," Sam grumbled. "Let me make it plain to you, Four. If what you're saying about where you...come from...is true, then I can understand that you're only acting on...on instinct right now." She hesitated, as if trying to determine the best way to explain. "But you...you can't just force yourselves on us. How would you like it if someone tried to force themselves on you? Someone bigger and stronger?"

As though Sam's words had struck home, Four's eyebrows shot upward. He cut a black glance at his twin. "Bal'four," he said in an ugly voice.

Both men stilled.

"Bal'four?" Jerri queried as she brushed a thumb over Deuce's nipple.

With lightning reflexes, Deuce clamped a hand around her wrist as his eyes widened. Slowly, he pulled her hand to his lips. "Bal'four," he nodded seriously. "Bal'four wouldn't leave Kar'four alone. He was always trying to...force my brother. Bal'four was huge."

Sam stared up at Four as her eyes softened. "I'm sorry," she said automatically.

Kar'four shrugged. "Don't be. I ended up breaking his wrist." His eyebrows moved together as he considered Sam's delicate wrist. "Are you...going to try to break my wrist?" He searched her eyes seriously.

Sam smiled. "Uh, no."

He smiled back. "That's just as well. Because I don't think it would work."

"The point is," Sam continued, "that you need to...ask first."

"Well," Deuce interrupted in another annoying drawl. "I can tell you what his next question will be."

"*And*," Jerri cut in, "it's customary for two people to get to know one another before they start ripping their clothes off. Before two people get to that point, they want to know something about each other. *If* we take this any farther, there are a few things Sam and I would want to know first. We'd want to know where you're from, for instance. What you're like. What you're doing here. Why you wear those masks. We'd want to know *if we liked you*."

"Oh," Deuce frowned grimly. "Well that's fucking awkward."

"Why?" Jerri asked as her eyes narrowed suspiciously.

Pulling away from Jerri, Deuce scraped a hand back through his midnight hair. "I agree that we probably owe you some explanations but they're going to be hard for us to pull off, in our current state." He looked down at his cock. "To be honest, I think the explanations would be easier to work through *after* we got fucked." He returned his troubled gaze to Jerri's face.

"You said you were from the future," Jerri prompted him while she had this narrow opening.

"The future," Deuce echoed vaguely as his gaze burned across the inches separating him from Jerri.

"Give him a minute," Four stated wryly. "I'm sure he'll come up with something...eventually."

Deuce turned his face slightly to scowl at his twin. "The future," he repeated, shaking his head as if to clear it. "Yes. We've traveled backward through time from the year 2250. And," he said, throwing back his shoulders. "We're prepared to prove it."

"We are?" Four asked, his surprise obvious.

"We are," Deuce stated firmly. "Because while *you* were reading *"How to Fuck a Real Woman in the Twenty-first Century,* I was studying Twenty-first Century History."

"And?" Four demanded, sounding impatient.

Deuce looked back to Jerri. "What's the date again?"

She blinked at him once. "Um…July twenty-third."

"On July twenty-third," Deuce stated confidently, "the Cubs beat the White Sox seven to one."

"You know the results of tonight's baseball game?" Jerri snorted. "Typical. Evidently men haven't changed *that* much in the future." Then Jerri stopped. "Wait a minute. You *know* the results of tonight's game?" Jerri slanted a sharp look toward Sam, her eyes bright with sudden realization. "Are you thinking what I'm thinking?"

"That depends," Sam said as she slowly smiled. "Are you thinking that we know the outcome of tonight's baseball game *and* we're in New Las Vegas, gambling capitol of the world?"

Jerri stared at Sam, her palms damp as the reality of what was happening here began to sink in. With a deep breath burning in her lungs, she gazed carefully around the opulent bedroom, taking in the small details that affirmed the extravagant luxury of Janus Palace, even in these cheaper floors in the clouds, which obscured the views of the electric city one hundred sixty floors below. Lush, thick sapphire carpet cushioned her feet, while a mammoth sleigh bed etched with the Greek key design stood with palatial grace off to her right, angled into the far corner, beside the floor to ceiling windows with their sheer curtains of ivory silk. Her meager wardrobe was housed in the tall mahogany chest braced against the wall behind Sam and Kar'four, its wooden surface gleaming with a rich, brilliant sheen of elegance and Jerri couldn't help the small part of her that yearned for the wealth to possess a room such as this for her own. And thanks to the man at her side, that possibility now seemed within her grasp.

"Yeah, Sam, that's exactly what I'm thinking. We freaking *know* the results of the world series," Jerri murmured thickly, waving her hand at her face as her cheeks regained their crimson burn. Her head nearly spun as the all-but-negative balance of her checkbook flashed before her eyes, her finances severely depleted after she'd scraped every dime of her savings to throw in with Sam for the convention space downstairs. "My God, we could make millions!"

"Mere millions?" Kar'four murmured, arching his expressive brows, while Deuce grabbed Jerri's arm and tugged her back to his side. "I'm afraid we can't let you do that," he laughed softly, lifting her pale hand to his mouth again and running his lips over her delicate knuckles.

Together, the two women narrowed their gazes at the grinning giant. "Why not?" Jerri demanded, blowing a breath of air up at the fringe of bangs hanging over her left eye.

"Jerri," he said, smiling tenderly as he rubbed his thumb over the soft flush of heat in her cheek "You've no need to worry about money anymore. We're hardly poor men."

Once again, the two friends moved in unison, their spines straightening as if jerked upward by a string, faces wearing identical, uncomfortable frowns. "And we're hardly whores," Sam finally stated, her normally husky voice as flat as her expression.

"And you've put words in my mouth," Deuce sighed, glaring at Sam as he shoved the long, clean fingers of his right hand through his thick, midnight hair, his left arm wrapping around Jerri's waist and securing her against his front. "I hope you don't plan on making a habit of it."

At Sam's side, Four snickered while she muttered, "Fine. What are you trying to tell us, then? And in case it escaped your notice, you were as naked as jaybirds when you landed or poofed or whatever the hell you call that stunning entrance you made in the convention center back there. Unless you have your millions crammed somewhere that I *don't* wanna know about, I don't think your so-called money is ever going to help us much here in 2050."

"I assure you the money of which I speak is not *in* my body at this time. And you'll be relieved to know that it's a good deal more accessible," Deuce teased with an endearingly crooked smile, "but we'll deal with that later. First we're going to discuss the fact that your bets, if you placed them, would be cheating."

Sam's lips parted but Kar'four stalled her words by holding up his hand. His dark hair fell forward as he lowered his head to murmur in her ear, the metal of his mask burning cool against her sensitive skin. "Look, regardless of what you think, he's right, Sam. There's no way you'd actually make that bet."

One honey-brown brow arched in amazement as she turned to stare at the stranger studying her through the thick line of his lashes. "And you know that *how*? We've only just met, you dolt! You hardly know a thing about me, other than the fact you'd like to get in my pants."

"And make you come," he added, nodding, while the ghost of a devilish grin twitched at the corner of his lips.

"What?" she rasped, shaking her head as if to clear it from a thick, heavy fog.

"You accused me of wanting to get in your pants, which is obvious to anyone with a set of eyes but you forgot the rest of it," he explained, his wicked blue eyes burning with mischievous delight. "Getting *in* you isn't going to be nearly enough, Sam. I want in and once there I want to *feel* what it's like to bring a beautiful woman to pleasure and have her body suck at mine, close around me like a fist and wring me of—"

"All right, damn it, I get it," Sam cut in, shoving him in the arm, then shaking out her hand when he didn't so much as budge. "Anything else?"

"Yeah," he said in a low, sin-rich whisper that stroked her senses like a forbidden pleasure. "The sooner you admit you want it too, the better," he growled playfully, while Jerri laughed softly under her breath.

"I hate to admit it, considering how badly we need that damn money, but he's right, Sam," Jerri conceded. "It's the same as when you wouldn't cheat off my geography test whenever Mr. Carlson would slam us with a pop quiz back in high school. Even after you'd been up all night taking care of your mom, you still refused to cheat." A soft sigh escaped the tightness of her throat. "As much as I'd like to cash in on this miracle, I guess we both know it isn't going to happen."

Sam glared at Jerri, then swung her gaze back to the waiting male at her side. "Yeah, well, that still doesn't explain how *he* knows it."

"Let's just say that we have good...*senses*." Four paused for a moment, studying her with his piercingly blue eyes and Sam could have sworn she felt something hungry crawl to life inside her skin, stretching and eager to pounce.

She licked her lower lip, fighting the urge to fan her face as Jerri had and seriously debating whether she needed to learn more about this hunk...or if she should just give in and grab him, shove him through the connecting doorway to her own room and jump his gorgeous bones until they either died from exhaustion or achieved nirvana. "What...er...what kind of senses?" she asked, forcing her mind to focus on something other than her killer case of lust and his badass bod.

Something moved through his eyes—something mysterious and dark—and her body answered with a warm, wet unfurling that made her want to melt on the spot. "I can't tell you," he said carefully. "At least not yet."

Shooting a quick look at Jerri, she crossed her arms and said, "Uh-uh. Talk...or we walk."

Making a frustrated sound in the back of his throat, Four's big hands landed on the lean line of his hips, his erection proud and impressively prominent as it surged through the open front panels of his duster. His dark, hard body seemed an endless, muscled landscape of rigid planes and sculpted curves. "Is that right?" he rasped, the words rolling off his tongue in a slow, taunting drawl.

Sam struggled to pull her tongue off the roof of her mouth as she eyed his imposing, yet mouthwatering equipment, her fuzzy, lust-dazed mind distantly aware of Jerri giggling softly on the other side of the room. "Um…yeah."

"I think we can change your mind."

"Oh yeah? And are you going to explain to us about the masks?" she asked, gesturing to the silver metal that obscured the upper right half of his face.

His grin flattened for a moment and he cut a sharp look at Deuce. "Later…"

Sam shook her head. "Uh-uh. Now."

"Look," he growled out on a tense, harsh breath. "We'll explain about the masks but you need to give us time."

"For what?" Jerri argued, her soft brown eyes moving from twin to twin, seeking an answer.

"We can't say," Deuce muttered somewhat miserably. "We can explain everything else. Just don't ask us to remove the masks."

"Why not?"

"Because you wouldn't understand what you saw beneath them."

"Jesus! Exactly what *can* you say that we would understand?"

"We're here for a reason," he offered tensely.

"A purpose," Four added.

"A mission?" Sam asked.

"Yes," the two men said in perfect unison. Four shared a speaking glance with Deuce and then said, "Two days from now, on July twenty-fifth, there's going to be a theft."

"Where?" the two women demanded at the same time.

"Here, in Janus Palace," Deuce explained. "We've been sent to stop it."

"And what are you supposed to do 'til then?" Sam laughed, shaking her head at their outrageous tale. "Copulate with any willing female you happen to come across?"

Four's answering smile was swift and eager and boyish. "We're only interested in *two* willing females and I have a whole slew of suggestions as to what we should do with them."

"Look, Conan," Sam snorted. "We're not going to bump bunnies with you and make the sloppy sixty-nine sea snake until we understand more about what's going on here."

"Bump bunnies?" Deuce snickered, while Four scratched his chin in thought, drawling, "Sloppy sixty-nine sea snake? Is that anything like that last story I read in Erotic Weekly? The one where the vampire and the librarian fuck themselves silly on top of the check-out counter?"

"Wow," Jerri giggled, her bright eyes shining with laughter. "You really *did* do your research."

"They did it sixty-nine times?" Deuce grunted, sounding stunned by the boggling concept. "Ten or so a night, I could see, with a woman like Jerri. *But sixty-nine?* Vampire or not, his fucking dick would've fallen off!"

"No, you moron," Kar'four snorted. "Didn't you listen to anything I tried to tell you about the sexual texts? The number sixty-nine refers to the *positions* of their bodies, not the number of times the act is carried out. The male puts his head between the woman's legs and eats her while she sucks him off."

"You've got to be kidding," Deuce scoffed, then drew up short when Four just shook his head and smiled. Cutting his brilliant gaze to Jerri, he eyed her with hot, fascinated interest. "Are real women *really* that flexible?" he asked hoarsely.

Kar'four shrugged his wide shoulders. "From what I've read they are."

"And what of their…taste? I made the mistake of licking a Synnie once." A slight shudder vibrated down his hard frame. "A week later, I could still taste hydraulic fluid."

Both Sam and Jerri choked on sudden barks of laughter, while Four arched his dark brow. "Well, according to the historical sexual texts, oral sex can be one of the most pleasurable acts a couple can share."

Deuce's hot blue eyes locked onto Jerri and moved slowly over her flushed body from head to foot before settling possessively on the plump vee between her thighs. "Damn," he grated out in a husky rasp, "this just keeps getting better and better."

Chapter Three
Everything Warm and Beautiful

ഌ

Wearing a warm, wicked, purely mischief-made smile, Deuce threw back his broad shoulders and shrugged as his long black duster slid down his muscled arms and puddled on the floor at his feet.

Jerri gasped softly, the small sound almost lost beneath the other couple's gently panting breaths as Sam and Kar'four *watched* her *watching* Deuce. Or maybe watching was putting it too lightly. Actually, she thought, stifling a low groan, her greedy stare probably fell more under the category of blatantly "eating him up" but there wasn't a damn thing she could do about it. He looked too deliciously damn edible. Like a bear drawn to the sweet, inexorable pull of fresh, luscious honey, Jerri's gaze fell to Deuce's groin where his thick erection sprang out of the curls that gathered in a dark, rich nest between his legs. With only a twinge of self-consciousness, she touched the center of her upper lip with her tongue and enjoyed a heady fantasy where she trailed her lips around the large, gleaming head of his cock.

Deuce stood unnaturally still as she drank in her visual fill of him, until he growled playfully and reeled Jerri toward him. He was all smooth, naked man and it was all she could do to stifle another heartfelt groan.

With a deep groove wedged between his brows, he frowned down at her chest. "Why do you wrap yourselves up in all this cloth?" he complained huskily as he picked away at the buttons of her shirt.

"Why do you insist on running about in nothing but your skin?" she countered breathlessly. All too aware of the fact that her body was a far cry from the mouthwatering perfection of his, her fingers flew to redo the work he'd undone.

Sam snorted behind her. "Haven't you seen *The Terminator*?" she reminded her friend. "You can't take anything with you through the time continuum," she stated with a know-it-all air of superiority. "When it comes to time travel, you have to go naked."

Deuce shot Sam a laughing look of surprise. "You've been watching way too much old science fiction," he told her, his blue eyes flashing with humor. "We arrived here naked because we left naked. In our time, we don't wear...all this fabric wrapped around our bodies."

Sam gave him a stunned look. "Why not?"

He shrugged. "We don't need it."

Jerri looked him over, head to foot, then frowned. "Even if humans have completely lost their inhibitions in the future, wouldn't it get a bit cold at times?"

"It isn't cold."

"It isn't...but what about the people who live in the northern latitudes?"

Deuce's face became suddenly grim. "There aren't any people in the North anymore. Or at least damn few. Mountain men. Pioneers. Everyone who's left lives in a band around the equator."

"Everyone who's *left*?" Jerri asked carefully as her fingers paused in the task of wrestling closed another button. "What do you mean?"

He raised his eyebrows regretfully as he cast a glance at Four.

"Well," Kar'four took up slowly, "there are no women in our time, to begin with. No *real* women. And not a lot of men either."

"No women at all?"

32

"Let me explain. On July twenty-fifth, 2050—two days from now—Janus Palace was robbed of two valuable masks. The masks were made of a very rare element."

"Mercoldium," Sam said.

"That's right," Four answered as he smiled down at her. A glow of golden light curled and wavered on the warm silver that hugged his cheekbone, wrapped his right eye and traced his hairline. The molded metal appeared to flow across his face in a thick pour of rich silver. "The masks were...*are* here in Janus Palace. Sixty seconds after they were stolen, a security program was set into motion. In response to the casino's security measures, lights came on throughout the palace, all exit doors were locked, barring escape, and...a gas was released at the location of the theft. The gas was supposed to be a harmless biological agent meant to render the thieves unconscious. It didn't work. The thieves threw a chair through a window and escaped with their treasure." Four took a deep breath before he continued. "The gas seeped throughout the palace before it dissipated. No one thought it was dangerous. But it was. It was deadly. Subject to heat and pressure over many years, the gas stored in the pressurized canisters had mutated into a dangerously infectious virus. When the gas was released, it initiated the most deadly plague of all time.

"The plague had an incubation period of a week. So seven days passed before anyone showed any symptoms of distress—ten before anyone died. By then, thanks to air travel, the plague had traveled around the world. The disease was gender specific. It targeted females. The women died before a vaccine or treatment could be developed," he explained. "All of them. Within three months, every single human female on the planet was dead. Every matriarch. Every mother. Every little girl." Kar'four cleared his throat, swallowed, then tried to continue again. Silently, he shook his head.

Jerri exchanged a look of horror with her best friend as Deuce's arm tightened around her. He pulled her close and Jerri felt herself melting against him as his lips skimmed across her forehead. "But we're here to stop all that," he stated tersely, giving her a reassuring squeeze.

"But," Sam argued tenaciously, "if all the females were wiped out in 2050, then how can there still be men in 2250? How were you...*born*?"

Deuce nodded as his eyes shifted with a guilty blue slide of color. "Almost immediately, scientists set to work trying to clone and recreate women. But the women they cloned could only survive in sterile isolation units. The plague persisted in the earth's atmosphere. The women they'd cloned couldn't have any contact with the outside world—any contact with men—and live. As the surviving generation of males aged, the scientists realized they'd have to clone men to continue the human race. That's what they've been doing ever since— cloning a small population of males to inhabit the planet while they looked for a way to undo the past.

"Last year saw a breakthrough in shattering the time barrier. Scientists sent a man back in time—the first Oranaut went back an hour, then a day. After a year of experimentation, the scientists felt they were ready to put someone back in 2050. We represent that first attempt."

Kar'four lifted his hand and tucked Sam's honey-stranded hair behind her ear. "We're here to change the past. We're going to stop the theft and save womankind."

Sam gazed up into his dark, soulful eyes. "And the masks you wear on your faces?" she persisted, her voice gentle.

Behind her, Deuce laughed—a harsh sound edged with bitterness. "Consider them a sort of punishment if you must, a symbol of man's evils—the price man paid to continue his humanity, thanks to that idiot Jane-us who killed off everything warm and beautiful in the world...for the sake of two cold, metal masks."

"Kar'four?" Sam asked softly.

"The explanation for our masks will just have to wait," Four murmured as he purposefully lowered his lips to hers.

As Four's lips sealed against her own, his strong hands clutching possessively at her upper arms, bringing her firmly against him, Sam mumbled, "Bwut whatta 'bout thew wobbery?"

With a low groaning sound of frustration in the back of his throat, he lifted his mouth no more than a fraction, his breath stirring gently with her own. "What?"

Gasping for air, Sam slowly blinked his gorgeous face into focus. "I said...but what about the robbery?"

"What about it?" he asked between nibbling bites to the corner of her kiss-swollen lips.

"Uh...shouldn't we all be searching or something?" Sam asked distractedly, already tilting her chin to give him better access to the sensitive skin beneath the edge of her jaw.

He paused once again at her words, lifting his dark head to stare intently into her eyes. "What do you mean *we*?"

"We...*us*," she enunciated slowly. "You know, the four people in this room. You and me and Deuce and Jerri." When he only continued to stare, a strange smile hovering deliciously at one corner of his wide mouth, she narrowed her eyes. "Don't tell me you thought we'd bail on you after what you've just told us. That we wouldn't help! What kind of crap is that?" she demanded, working herself up while he just continued to stare, that strange smile growing in intensity, curling softly across his devastating mouth.

Laughing warmly, he pressed his lips to hers again, quickly then kissed his way to her ear. "I'm not admitting to anything that's going to piss you off —"

"Smart man," Deuce called out from the other side of the room, where he held a grinning, blushing Jerri firmly against his very naked, very aroused body.

"So," Four growled, glaring at his brother before he smiled back down at Sam, "I'll just say that I'm more than *honored* you're willing to help us." He lifted his hand to brush her fallen hair back from her face once again, curling his palm against her cheek in a tender gesture that made something deep inside Sam's tummy do another one of those warm-fuzzy kind of flips. "You're a truly fascinating woman, Sam Hayward."

She snickered softly, laughing now as she said, "That's just because you don't *know* any others."

"Wouldn't matter, sweetheart. I have a feeling Deuce and I, to use a locally appropriate phrase, *hit the jackpot* when we met you two." His smile reached the liquid blue of his eyes and her knees damn near buckled at the devastating combination of heat and blossoming affection smoldering there. "I'm warning you now," he whispered, lowering his mouth to hers once again, "that I'm going to kiss you and this time, *I'm...not...stopping.*"

On the other side of the room, Jerri and Deuce shared a knowing smile. Jerri nodded her head toward the door that led to the other room, which was actually Sam's, though it didn't appear that Sam was going to remember that fact anytime soon. The thought made her grin with devilish delight, more than glad that her best friend was finally having her socks knocked off—and by such a gorgeous hunk at that.

Not that she didn't have her own hunk vying for her attention—and that thought changed her grin from devilish to downright carnal. Deuce's own playful smile faltered at the change, that raging fire retaking his gaze, hot and possessive as it moved over her from head to foot and back up again. Jerri quickly gave him her back, afraid she might cry out in need from nothing more than his blasted look—though as far as looks went, it was a killer. The kind that said he wanted to lay her out, spread her open and purposefully subject her lucky bod to all manner of raw, wicked, sexually explicit pleasures.

Hell yes!

Biting her lower lip to keep from squealing with the excitement pumping through her veins, Jerri began walking just that little bit faster.

They made it silently across the room, careful not to break the magic of the kiss consuming Sam and Kar'four, until finally the connecting door clicked shut behind them and the most gorgeous man she'd ever set eyes on turned to stare at her from the center of the opulent bedroom.

"*Jaysus,*" Jerri whispered, touching her palms to the burning heat in her cheeks, her starved gaze glued to the hard proof of his mutual desire as it stood up proud and demanding from the dark nest of curls in his groin.

"Jerri," he said in a rough, whiskey-rich rumble of sound. "Come here."

Yes, that was a freaking brilliant idea but for some bizarre-ass reason completely at odds with her sex-hungry inner wild woman, she heard herself say, "I still don't understand how—"

"You don't have to," he cut in, taking a step closer. "I swear, I'll explain everything you want to know—answer all your questions—just *later.*"

"But this is important and—"

He broke her off with a hard, rumbling laugh as he moved quickly before her. Taking her cool hand into the vivid warmth of his own, he wrapped her fingers around the burning heat of his cock and said, "It's not nearly as important as *this.*" His fingers squeezed and his cock pulsed hard within her hold. "Take mercy on me, Jerri, before I fucking die here."

She stared down at him in her hand, her blood seeming to move faster…thicker through her veins when she realized she couldn't even touch her fingers around his deliciously firm width. "I think maybe you're right," she groaned, squeezing her fingers until the thick roping of veins bulged and he growled a low, dark animal sound in the back of his throat.

"Jerri," he rasped, the sound of his voice like dry, fire-colored leaves beneath your feet in fall, crackling and sharp.

She wet her mouth, wishing she were wetting *other* things. "Yeah?"

Tilting up her chin until she met his heavy gaze, the deep blue shadowed by the thick fringe of his lashes, he said, "Lose the clothes, sweetheart."

And just like that, Jerri felt some of her internal heat go cool. "I'm...well, I'm not a synthetic, Deuce. I won't be perfect and beautiful," she explained, her voice low and uncomfortable. "Not...not like you."

His head tilted as he studied her in a way that clearly said she was his entire focus, that he wanted her much more than she could ever imagine. "Jerri, there isn't a woman alive, whether she's synthetic or real, who could possibly be more desirable to me than you are."

"Oh," she sighed, then shook her head as she felt herself falling under his spell. "I...uh, bet that any man who'd never seen a *real* woman before would probably think that," she teased softly, surprised when instead of smiling, his hard look flashed with angry frustration.

"Bullshit. Do you think I didn't notice the attention back there?" he asked, crowding into her until she had to crane her neck back at an awkward angle to be able to hold his glare. "I could've had *any* one of those women with a snap of my fingers, with the ease of a smile, but none of them interested me."

She shook her head in confusion, then almost burst out laughing when she realized they were arguing while she still held a death grip on his massive, glorious erection. "I don't understand you," she whispered, while her hand possessively stroked him from root to tip.

"Are we going to argue over why I'm so attracted to you or are you going to shut up and let me prove just how desirable I find you?" he demanded in a low, hoarse rumble, while his mouth curled once again into that devastatingly sexy grin that made her heart stutter every damn time. "You, Jerri. Not some stick with balloons on her chest. Not some scientist's creation of perfection. *You*," he whispered, lifting his hands to cradle her cheeks in his palms. "Soft and warm and real and so impossibly fucking sexy."

"Um…I guess I'm just going to shut up."

He laughed, a dark, deep erotic sound, and gently kissed her forehead. "Do you know what I want first?" His voice was soft, his rough-silk lips moving sweetly against her skin even softer.

A faint, nervous giggle broke free from her chest. "I'm almost afraid to guess."

"As much as I'm eager to know the feel of your sweet little pussy," he said, his smile warm and wicked. "To know how snug and hot it's going to fit me—first, I want to learn what it *tastes* like. First, I want to fuck it with my tongue, sweetheart."

"God have mercy," she said so softly that it was little more than an awed whisper of sound.

One dark brow arched while his blue eyes flashed with lust and anticipation, the corners crinkling sexily as he sent her a truly mischief-born smile. "You like the idea?"

"Let's just say that if you don't hurry up," she panted, feeling everything inside her clench with need and a physical hunger unlike anything she'd even known, "I'll be crossing the finish without you."

"Oh honey, we can't have that," he laughed out on a low, keen rumble…and before she could blink, the magnificent hunk dropped to his knees before her.

Chapter Four
All I Can Think About is Sex

சு

How she got to be *here*, in *this* whopper of a situation, Jerri wasn't certain she could explain. A quick rundown of the facts didn't seem any more believable than the idea of such a gorgeous guy—not to mention intelligent, compassionate and so eager for her that his mouthwatering cock looked like it would erupt any second now—down on his knees in front of her.

Of a guy like *that* getting ready to go down on her.

Damn, she whispered within her mind, *I must be luckier than I thought.*

It seemed inconceivable and yet there he was, with his dark head just inches away, dreamy blue eyes focused right there between her legs, that beautiful face hovering just inches away from her denim-covered crotch.

She drew a shaky breath as his large hands lifted, making short work of her button and zipper—then forgot to breathe altogether when those same rugged hands grasped the waist of her jeans and began pulling. He maneuvered them down carefully, gently over her hips, her thighs, moving so slowly, until his patience suddenly broke and in some kind of seamless Jiu-Jitsu move, he had her flat on her back, the jeans clearing her ankles and her white lace panties shredding beneath the desperate grip of his hands.

Then he was pushing her legs apart, spreading her thighs wide, *staring at her right there* and everything in Jerri's body seemed to clench and swell with sharp, raw-edged anticipation.

"So beautiful," he rasped, those impossibly strong hands digging into the soft flesh of her inner thighs and pushing harder, forcing them wider, every shaky movement allowing her to see just how much he needed her — wanted her — all of it blazing in that pure blue gaze as he ate her up with an almost savage visual appetite. "I can't decide where to start."

She couldn't help the rough laugh that broke from her throat. "Uh…anywhere will be great, Deuce. Trust me."

"But I want to be everywhere at once," he laughed, grinning, his voice coming low and gruff with excitement. "Everywhere," he added thickly and she felt the first stroke of one callus-tipped finger touch the ripened bud of her clit, then delve slowly down the thick, wet seam of her labia, opening her up.

"Oh god…what are you doing?" she gasped, knowing very well what he was about but needing to keep talking to avoid begging him to fuck her already.

His answer came in the slow, wicked smile curving across his mouth, though his eyes never left the tingling flesh between her legs that now felt so exposed, so naked and wet and vulnerable beneath that smoldering, tactile stare.

God, it was beyond intimate, beyond anything Jerri had ever experienced, the way he just kept *looking* at her. With intense focus, he watched the movement of his finger as he petted her puffy outer lips, then her sensitive vulva, circling her pulsing clit before dipping the thick tip into her tight opening, his eyes going hazy with pleasure at that first feel of her pussy clutching around him.

"I could eat you alive, Jerri," he whispered huskily, taking a slow, deep breath into his lungs as if she was the sweetest thing he'd ever known. "I'm going to tongue-fuck this sweet little cunt until you come all over my face, woman. Until you scream and shout and I can feel your pussy sucking on my tongue the same fucking way it's gripping my finger."

"Oh god...Deuce, now," she groaned, gripping his broad, sweat-slick shoulders as he leaned closer, his hot breath pelting her tender, intimate flesh. "Please! *Oh please...oh please...*"

"Is that how you say it, Jerri? A tongue-fuck?" he asked, a wicked gleam in his deep blue eyes as he shot a quick glance up at her face, his look saying he knew exactly how much she wanted his mouth on her.

Like there's any hiding that, she thought with an inner snicker.

"Oh yeah, that'll do," she moaned, breathing hard. And if his look was any indication, about to breathe even harder.

"You'll tell me if I do it wrong," he said, the words sounding like both an arrogant order and an endearing request. And then, suddenly, he was lifting her into his powerful arms and taking her to the foot of the bed, where he playfully tossed her onto the high, luxurious mound of down-filled bedding.

Tenderness damn near broke her heart. "Deuce, you could just stare at me and I swear I'd melt."

"But I want to do so much more than look," he confessed in a silky rasp, his strong hands positioning her limbs just how he wanted her, the soft light streaming through the sheer curtains shimmering on the metallic surface of his mask. "You're so soft and pink," he growled, ripping at the buttons of her shirt and pulling down the cups of her bra, baring her plump nipples, before suddenly plunging two long, thick fingers into her needy pussy. "And wet. Damn, Jerri, you're melting for me, all slippery and tight, and I can't wait anymore."

One second she was moaning and in the next Deuce's ears were filled with the rough, sobbing sounds of animal pleasure breaking out of her as he opened his eager mouth over the wet heat of her cunt and learned, for the first time in his life, what it felt like to have his face buried in a beautiful, delicious, fucking, mind-blowing little pussy.

The pure eroticism of the act nearly killed him—the intoxicating taste, feel and scent of her no doubt addicting him for life.

The outside world became a dull, distant buzzing in his ears, while his reality centered down to the raw sound of her cries and the exquisite perfection of stroking his tongue through all that slick, slippery juice that reminded him of sun-ripened peaches. Of curling his tongue around that thrumming little heartbeat at the top of her cleft and suckling. Putting his tongue as far into her clenching little opening as he could reach. The pure thrill of tongue-fucking her to the point that she trembled upon the bed, muscles quivering, while her hands gripped the dark strands of his hair and held him to her, demanding more. And then that ultimate moment when he closed his mouth over her clit and shoved three thick fingers up into her—hard—fucking and sucking in an instinctual rhythm that had her stiffening…screaming…and then pulsing, clenching, rippling around his fingers until her juices covered him up to his wrist, his face damp with her and that hot wash of cum slipping gently from her tender cunt tempting him beyond reason. With a carnal snarl of sound, he pulled his fingers free and fastened his lips over that clenching opening, thrusting his tongue deep, swallowing as he took in as much of her sweet, rich release as he could. Over and over again he drew from her, feeding off her liquid pleasure, until she went limp beneath him, the soft, hitching sounds of her breath matching the slow tremors still coursing through her sated body.

Deuce lifted his head and moved slightly higher over her quivering form, until he could rest his hot face against her trembling belly, his lungs working hard for air, muscles clenched tight against the violent needs of his body.

He was lost in her. There was no other way to describe the strange, foreign, almost terrifying emotions struggling for dominance in his warrior's mind. Lost to his find, mesmerized by discovery, not because it was so new, but because of *her*.

He was lost in the woman. Lost in Jerri.

Lifting his head, Deuce raised his gaze to the beauty of her face. Her dark hair lay in a wild, tangled halo around her head, one long strand of dark silk caught across her damp cheek, skin flushed with the warm burn of pleasure overload. She was so beautiful that his gut clenched and with purposeful, carnal intent, he began kissing his way up her soft, smooth body, losing himself for long, blissful moments in the sweet bounty of her breasts, nearly undone by the erotic feel of her soft, pink nipples in his mouth…of suckling at her in pure, ravenous abandon.

Only when he felt the last shreds of his hard-worn control completely slipping did he force himself higher, positioning his knees between her thighs, upper body braced on one hand beside her head. Then he simply stared down into the luminous beauty of her thick-lashed eyes. She gave him a shy, sweet smile that melted his heart and he lifted one rough finger to gently stroke the soft curve of her cheek. "When you blush like that, you have the same pretty pink of your little pussy lips right here on your cheeks."

"Oh god," she said huskily, her dark gaze going heavy with want.

Deuce trailed his hand over her cheek, down her throat, to the soft swells of her breasts. "You are so fucking sweet, Jerri," he rasped, playing with one puckered nipple, then the other, loving how they instantly responded to his touch. "I swear by my Ocean Mother, I never knew anything could be so sweet."

With a low groan, he lowered his head to her breasts once more, capturing one swollen pink nipple between his lips, then hungrily drawing it into the blistering heat of his mouth, sucking and licking the sensitive nub, painting it with strokes of pleasure until she cried out, arching beneath him. Only then did he lift his head and stare down into her face as she panted,

"Deuce, not that this isn't wonderful...I mean, breathtakingly wonderful...but don't you...you know...?"

"What?" he asked, smiling wickedly, loving the way she blushed like an innocent temptress.

She chewed the corner of her full lower lip. "Wouldn't you rather —"

"Wouldn't I rather be fucking you right now?" he finished for her, his voice a low, scratchy slice of sound that seemed to echo the desperate, churning ache of need knotted in his dick.

"Yeah," she whispered, returning his smile.

"To be honest, Jerri, I want to fuck you so bad I can hardly see straight," he gritted out, shifting until he could shove himself against the wet heat of her sex in a hard, sliding motion that worked the rigid length of his cock along the thick, swollen seam of her labia, "but...there were things I wanted more first. Things...things I hadn't expected to want so badly."

Her head tilted to the side as she studied him. "What things?"

His head lowered the barest fraction, so that he was staring at her from beneath the thick screen of his lashes. "Your pleasure."

Her breath caught and he struggled to find the right words to express these newfound, somewhat unsettling emotions playing havoc with his equilibrium. "I wanted your...your comfort. I want you to feel *comfortable* with me. I didn't...I don't want you to feel —"

"Deuce," she said, her smile breathtaking, her soft hands stroking his lower back in a caring, tender caress, "you have to believe me when I tell you that I've never...*never* wanted a man more than I want you. Please trust me when I say that I want this as badly as you do."

For at least two seconds, Deuce hovered at Jerri's tender entrance, savoring her wet heat wrapped around the hungry, swollen crown of his cock. As he fought for control, his dick pulsed with need, feeding his first searing drop of cum into Jerri's warm channel.

He dragged his open mouth along her jawline to her ear. "Then I hope you're willing to bear my child," he whispered in a strained voice. "Because, after two hundred years without the sound of a child's laughter, I'm not about to stop what happens next."

A muffled pounding reached his ears, like thunder sounding in the distance and for a moment he wondered if the sound was his thundering heart beating wildly in his chest. He shook his head, concentrating on the mind-blowing feel of Jerri's sweet, slick pussy kissing the aching, insistently throbbing head of his dick.

Jerri's lips parted but her answering comment was lost in the hammering of a heavy fist on the door connecting the two rooms. "Deuce!" Four bellowed from the adjoining room. The loud, abrasive sound screeched down his nerve endings, making him grind his teeth.

"Deuce! Jerri! You two need to get over here," Four called out. "Now!"

He looked down at a wide-eyed Jerri and worked his jaw. "I'll fucking kill him," he snarled softly.

Jerri's normally soft brown eyes glittered with feminine outrage. "Not if I get to him first."

* * * * *

In an angry flash of movement, Deuce was on his feet and reaching for the door, ripping it open in a raging fury of energy. Taut-faced, Kar'four blinked into the room. His black duster hung from his shoulders, baring his chest, lower abdomen and his straining erection. Jerri squeaked as she rolled on the ivory duvet, wrapping the creamy eyelet coverlet around her pale hips and tugging it upward to hide her exposed breasts.

As Deuce glared at his brother, his cock bounced against his hard abdomen. His nettled flesh was tight and angry looking, his pre-cum, as well as Jerri's sweet moisture, cooling his tip. "What!" he barked at the tense face framed in the open doorway.

"The booth has been robbed," Kar'four ground out as though each word cost him a fortune in effort. "Sam and Jerri's booth. We've had a call on the—"

"Telephone," Sam's voice supplied from within the adjoining room.

"Telephone," Four growled, ripping his hand back through the black silk of his hair. "We have to go back down to the convention center and meet with some people. I— *By the Skies*, how close did you get?" he asked abruptly, forcing a rough breath through his clenched teeth.

"Not close enough. You?"

Kar'four shook his head distractedly. "She let me kiss her but then she just wanted to keep...*talking*. I...*Mother of Darkness*...I didn't know it would be like this," Four groaned softly, slumping against the doorframe. "I didn't know it would be so fucking hard to wait. If something doesn't happen soon," he muttered, casting his eyes back in Sam's direction, "I'm going to bang her upside the first flat surface I can find— horizontal, vertical or otherwise. What the hell have we gotten ourselves into, brother?"

Deuce just shook his head, knowing exactly what sort of hell Four was going through.

"I need this woman, brother. I need her *now*. I...we have a robbery to stop and all I can think about is sex."

"I know," Deuce told him quietly. "I know." Reaching out with one big hand, he wrapped it around the back of Four's neck and dragged his brother's forehead forward to touch his own. "Pull yourself together, man. First things first. We'll deal with this problem downstairs," he stated resolutely, as they shared a moment of brotherly commiseration. "Then we'll get fucked. And we'll make sure they do it to within an inch of our lives, Four. Until we can't even remember our bloody names." Pulling his face away a few inches, Deuce gave his brother a hard smile. "Okay?"

Kar'four jerked his chin upward in answer, trying for but not quite pulling off an answering grin.

"Give us a second," Deuce told his brother. "Jerri will want to—"

"Get dressed," Jerri finished for him.

Deuce nodded, looking none too pleased by the statement.

"And you guys are going to have to cover your hides as well," she threw at the two men. Rolling off the bed with the froth of eyelet pulled up into her cleavage, Jerri stooped to dig through a large cardboard box on the floor. "These should do," she murmured, as she surveyed a long pair of button-fly jeans, frowned at the men in the doorway, then returned her attention to the vintage denim-wear. With a quick nod, she tossed first one pair of jeans at the twins, then a second pair.

The men shook the jeans out as they considered them doubtfully. "How," Deuce said finally, his eyes narrowed on his raging hard-on, "am I going to get all of *this* stuffed into these things?"

"My question, exactly," Kar'four muttered, while his brows pulled together into a tight frown.

Sam poked her head into the room. "We'll help. Won't we, Jerri?"

Watching Sam's gaze settle on the purpled head of his cock, Four groaned. "This is going to take a while," he predicted.

Laughing, Sam pulled Four back into the room and pushed him at the bed. As he dropped into a sitting position on the edge of the mattress, the fingers of his right hand automatically curled loosely around his erection, casing it in the open cage of his fist.

"Don't do that," she told him, slapping his hand.

"Do what?"

"Don't hold your cock like that. It's provocative."

His mouth drew out into a tense line as he stroked his hand up his length from root to tip. "Good," he muttered darkly.

Dropping to her knees, Sam yanked the faded jeans out of his grasp and bunched the legs up before pulling the pants over his feet. "Sorry we don't have any shorts for you," she apologized.

"What are shorts?"

She hesitated. "Another layer of clothing," she finally decided.

"Then I wouldn't want them," he bit off.

"No," Sam mused as she knelt before him and worked the jeans up his legs. "I don't suppose you would. Stand up," she told him.

"You're a bossy little bitch," he complained as he got to his feet and she worked the jeans up his flanks to his waist then stared frowningly at his erection pushing out through the open gap of his unbuttoned pants.

"It...uh...doesn't look like it's going to fit," she mumbled, swallowing the saliva that suddenly washed into the corners of her mouth.

"Probably not," he grated roughly. "At least, not while you're on your knees in front of me with your pretty pink mouth only inches away from my dick." His hands hovered uneasily at his sides as he glared down at her.

Slowly, she lifted her hands to the thick, fleshy rod. "Maybe I'll just..."

With those unfinished words, Sam wrapped one hand carefully around the base of his cock as she tried to guide the monster inside his jeans. As her fingers came into contact with the burning silk that covered his erection, Kar'four's hips jerked forward, a sharp hiss bursting past his lips. He blinked several times as he stared down at his cock in her hand.

Sam frowned worriedly, nibbling on her bottom lip. "Maybe I'll just...maybe I'll just..."

"Mother of Darkness," Kar'four rasped as he reached for the back of Sam's head and cradled it in his large palm. He pulled her face into his groin and pressed the damp heat of her mouth against the tautly stretched skin of his cock. "Sam!" he groaned, "Shut up and kiss me."

Chapter Five
Myth and Mystery

** හ**

Four closed his eyes in a brief prayer then opened them again to watch Sam's soft, full lips snuggled up against his erection. "Sam," he whispered, his voice warm with wonder as he watched the brassy little spitfire on her knees before him, apparently worshipping the straining flesh that sprang from the damp curls in his groin. As he gazed down on Sam's honey-brown hair, she tilted her head. Her eyes were half closed in an expression of tender adoration as she moved her mouth up his long, ridged length.

The moment she'd pressed her luscious lips against his shaft, she seemed to have shed her cool, offhand exterior. The transformation left him poised on that sharp, desperate edge of ultimate need. Seeing her bloom beneath the provocative heat of passion and hunger made him ache for fulfillment, for closeness, but most importantly, *for Sam*.

Four could only watch in amazement as she made love to his cock with her tongue and her lips. Her mouth was open, twisting against his tight skin, heating his aching flesh with the small bursting pants that caught in her throat. Stunned, Kar'four reached down with one finger to lift her chin. Caught unawares, her unshielded gaze revealed a wealth and depth of emotion he'd never have guessed at. The cool little hussy wanted him. She wanted him as much as he wanted her. It was written all over her face in molten lust.

His gut knotted with burning, nearly unbearable satisfaction and he reached for her.

In one swift move, Kar'four had her on the bed beneath him, thrusting between her legs before he even had her pants off. His hips moved instinctively, subject to a primitive male urgency that couldn't be tempered or directed.

"Fuck," he snarled in frustration, as he fought to get Sam's jeans open and down her legs.

"Kar'four."

"Fuck," he shouted again, ignoring his brother's voice behind him.

"Four!"

Kar'four shook his head, staring down into Sam's smoldering green gaze, groping for the tattered remnants of his control. Slowly, he turned his gaze toward his twin, who now stood in the doorway to the adjoining room.

"We're ready," Deuce told him.

Kar'four closed his eyes as he pulled in a groan that was weighted with suffering.

"You're the one who came hammering on *our* door," Deuce reminded his brother gruffly, "to tell us we have to go downstairs and meet with some people."

Four jerked his chin in acknowledgement, staring down into Sam's eyes, searching her gaze as sanity returned to her expression in small, careful degrees. He could have wept as her eyes shifted to focus on his chest and the warm green glow of feminine passion was replaced by something more familiar, something much cooler.

"No," he whispered with sudden vehemence. His fingers grasped her chin as he forced her to meet his gaze. "Don't you dare," he whispered. "Don't you dare go back there, Sam. Stay with me. I want you here with me!"

Her eyes flashed a moment in a brief surge of heat. Then it was gone. Whatever passion, whatever fire he'd managed to evoke in her for that brief instant was gone, buried once again beneath her cool exterior.

With a sigh so deep that it hurt, he shoved himself away from her and rolled off the bed. This time, when she reached for the metal buttons on his fly, he knocked her hands away. Without looking at her, he buttoned himself in. "Let's go," he told his brother.

Reaching for the door, Four yanked it open and stalked out into the corridor. When he reached the elevator, he punched the top button, realized that probably wasn't right, jabbed the bottom button with one finger then smacked the top button again in pure frustration. Hunching his shoulders, he shoved his hands in his pockets and turned his face away as his companions caught up to him. He was damned if he was going to look into those cool, impersonal green eyes again when he was wearing his own emotions on his fucking sleeve for everyone to see—for everyone to see every time he looked at her.

The elevator doors shushed open and he stepped inside to the right then moved to the back of the car, putting several people between himself and Sam. He stared at the flat metal doors that closed him inside the elevator. When they reached the convention center level, he was the last one out, sulking along several feet behind the other three with his eyes focused on the ground ahead of him.

A shoulder bumped into his as they made their way through the crowds toward Sam and Jerri's booth. He ignored it. He ignored the snicker that followed a few seconds later. But when a large hand wrapped around his biceps, he stopped and stared at the dirty, ragged nails of the thick, trespassing fingers. His eyes narrowed on the large fist locked on his arm as a loud voice boomed close to his ear. "Hey Princess! What's with the mask?"

Kar'four lifted his narrowed gaze to the face of a large, belligerent, quite possibly drunk mauler. Four's voice was like sliding steel. "Just to warn you," he growled, "the last man who grabbed my arm is still learning to write with his left hand."

The man's eyes shifted as his gaze widened in surprise.

Four gave him five seconds to make up his mind. He was about to act when the mauler loosed him with a shove. When Kar'four turned away, the man's taunting words followed him.

"What a fucking clown. Walking around New Vegas wearing a metal mask! Bet he's got a chastity belt to match."

Four froze in the middle of the crowd, lifting his gaze to meet his brother's.

"No!" Deuce shouted, lunging for Four's arm.

But it was too late. Kar'four whirled. With the big man's wrist in his fist, he pulled the man's arm and stretched it straight, twisting the wrist as he angled it toward his back. With the arm stretched to its limit, Four threw his knee upward. The big man howled as his ligaments tore at the elbow.

As Deuce rushed his brother away from the screaming man, Four caught a glimpse of Sam's stunned expression. He smiled, filled with grim satisfaction.

Jerri hurried to catch up as Sam followed the two men closely. "What the hell was that?" Sam shouted.

"Leave him," Deuce told her, stepping between Sam and his brother.

"Are you nuts? Are you two absolutely stark, barking mad? The man was backing down and—"

"Shut up, Sam." Deuce cut her off with a snarl. "Where we come from, you don't leave a man like that at your back. Where we come from, you're either strong or you're fucked."

"Well this isn't where you come from, Deuce! The guy was harmless. Kar'four overreacted."

"And whose fault is that?" Deuce blasted back at her. "Who left him strung out at the edge of reason, at the edge of sanity? You think it's funny what we're going through? You think it's a joke? *You* try living your entire life without the opposite sex and see what happens when you find yourself standing on the verge of a lifetime dream, staring at the chance to finally realize your deepest fantasies, only to have it yanked out from under your feet!"

Tense silence crackled in the space that separated Sam from Deuce while Jerri pulled herself against his arm, watching his face with wide, troubled eyes.

"Sex," Sam muttered defensively. "This isn't about anything but sex."

Deuce shook his head. "No, Sam," he said tiredly. "It's more than that. The dream — the fantasy — is more than that. It's the whole myth and mystery of a woman's love."

Like a deflating beach toy, the fight went out of Sam in a halting rush. Her shoulders slumped as she turned to face a tense Kar'four. "I'm sorry," she mumbled. "I'm sorry about what happened back there in the room."

Kar'four met her shielded gaze. "Yeah?" he growled sullenly, turning away from her, "well, you know what you can do with that."

Jerri watched Kar'four stalk away on long, muscular legs encased in vintage denim and knew that Sam couldn't take her eyes off him.

"Why's she fighting it so hard?" Deuce whispered in her ear as they watched Sam shake her head then move off in the direction Kar'four had taken through the crowd of conventioneers and gamblers. Deuce had lowered his head so that she could feel his warm breath against her sensitive skin, one powerful arm wrapped possessively about her shoulders and the rushing feeling of warmth and happiness that pulsed through Jerri was undeniable.

Man, you've got it so bad, girl, she thought with a shivery moan.

"I'm not really sure," she murmured softly, her concern for Sam the only thing dimming that strange pulse of happiness that came every time Deuce touched her, or spoke to her, or hell, even looked at her. Yep, she had it *bad, bad, bad.*

Jerking her attention back to the problem of Sam and Four, she said, "I think that maybe she's...afraid."

Deuce's brows drew together in a questioning frown. "Of Four? I know he comes on a little strong," he muttered and she could have sworn a bright spot of pink burned beneath the tanned skin that stretched tautly across his right cheekbone, "but there's no way in hell he'd ever hurt her or do something she didn't want him to do."

Jerri shook her head and reached down for his big hand, loving the way he curled those long, powerful fingers around her much smaller ones. It was a dominant hold and yet, one that seemed careful too, as if he knew he could hurt her and would die before doing it.

"I don't mean physically," she explained, pulling him along with her as she headed in the direction both Four and Sam had taken. The air was crisp and cool from overhead air conditioning vents and yet welcoming too, as the sumptuous scents of richly brewed coffee and freshly baked cinnamon rolls reached them from a nearby catering booth. Reminding herself that she should offer to feed the poor guy when they were finished there, Jerri tugged him along behind her. As they moved deeper into the crowd, she had to raise her voice to be heard as the noise level around them grew. "What I mean," she added, "is that she's not afraid of his size or his strength. It takes a lot to intimidate Sam physically."

Jerri looked back over her shoulder in time to see Deuce shoot her a skeptical look at that particular statement and she laughed softly. "It's true. You'd be surprised at what a little bad-ass Sam can be."

His beautiful mouth twisted with curious frustration, the bright sunshine spilling in through the far wall of windows gleaming sharply against the metallic surface of his mask, causing refracting arcs of light to paint his face in iridescent shafts of color. He was so incredibly gorgeous...and he was hers. It was such a yummy concept that she could barely believe it.

"If that's true, then why the hell is she afraid of him?"

"There are all different types of fear, Deuce. I think Sam is…being cautious toward Four because she doesn't trust him on an emotional level. This—everything happening here—is moving at warp speed and if Sam feels the same kind of…um, *attraction* for Four that I feel for you," she explained carefully, aware that she was blushing now, "then she's going to fight it at first. That's just the way she is." A proud smile curled around the corners of her mouth at the thought of all her friend had accomplished in her life and she said, "Sam's a fighter."

The deep pools of mysterious blue in his eyes still shimmered with a fraction of doubt but Jerri could see that he was at least trying to believe her. Her smile shifted into a mischievous grin, thinking of how fun it would be when Sam's killer skills were eventually put to the test and these warriors were given a glimpse of what a woman could actually be capable of.

"If Sam's a fighter," he murmured, "then what are you?" The words came in a warm, provocative rumble that Jerri felt ease beneath her skin, making her shiver with sensual awareness. Then his hand shifted around hers, his thumb stroking a slow, suggestive pattern against her dampening palm that had her melting between her legs, remembering the way that clever thumb had stroked other, more intimate parts of her body.

"Um," she all but croaked, delicately clearing her throat as she struggled to find her voice. "Um, I guess you could say that I'm a lover," she teasingly drawled, laughing when she heard him groan a low, purely masculine, anguished sound of arousal beneath his breath.

"You're a tease is what you are," he grunted. "Tempting me beyond control."

Jerri shot what she hoped was a sultry glance over her shoulder and fluttered her eyelashes. "Do I tempt you, Deuce?"

"Keep looking at me like that, angel," he softly growled, "and in about two seconds everyone here is going to know just how badly you tempt me when I strip those fucking jeans off your hot little ass and nail you to the fucking floor with my cock."

It took a moment before she was able to swallow the thick lump of lust in her throat. "Damn," she whispered, her voice husky with desire and he smiled wickedly in response.

The crowd thickened ahead of them and Jerri tried to politely work her way through with Deuce close behind her, the heat from his hot, hard, magnificent bod making her feel flushed. Or maybe that was just from their suggestive little exchange. Whatever it was, she had the feeling that if she didn't get him into a bed and soon, she just might let him *take* her in the middle of the friggin' convention floor. The thought would have made her snicker with amusement but a rude man with garlic breath bumped into her just then, stepping on her left foot, and she cried out in pain. Deuce pulled her to him, wrapped one arm securely about her waist and shoved the asshole out of their way with the other. Jerri was ready to push him in front of her and allow him to clear a path when she heard a shrill scream break out just ahead of them, followed by Sam's voice shouting out over the swelling chatter of the crowd and everyone around them rushed forward to see what the commotion was.

"Deuce, get us through there," she cried out and he was already moving in front of her, pushing bodies out of his way, clearing a path that led them to a small clearing before their booth. Reaching Deuce's side, Jerri immediately took in the situation and knew they were in deep shit.

Kar'four stood to the side of the booth, his muscular arms crossed over his chest, blue eyes narrowed and cool as he stared at Sam. Though he tried to mask his emotions, Jerri could clearly see that he wanted nothing more than to grab her best friend up and steal her away. It would have made her smile, if not for the fact that Sam was in no position to be carried off anywhere.

No, Jerri very much feared that her best friend was about to be arrested for public disturbance, not to mention assault, if something wasn't done before the situation got out of control.

Sam stood over the prone body of the same snooty blonde they'd encountered earlier that day, a thick plastic rod clutched in Sam's hands, one end pressed purposefully against the windpipe of the hysterically crying woman.

A quick glance into their booth revealed four starkly naked racks that had previously displayed their merchandise. The fifth one lay in pieces on the ground — except for the long spanning rod that Sam gripped in her hands.

"Deuce," Jerri hissed, "get that damn stick away from her!"

Deuce stared at Jerri, gave the whimpering blonde two seconds of attention and then cut a meaningful look at his brother, before finally turning back to Jerri with a look of "what do you want me to do" stamped across his rugged features.

She groaned under her breath and gave him another shove. "Deuce, don't argue," she muttered. "Just trust me. Sam is lethal with a staff. If you don't want her getting arrested, you'll get it away from her."

"Help me," the blonde gasped from her captive position on the floor, her mascara running into thick circles around her spite-filled baby blues, giving her the pitiful look of a raccoon. "God, somebody get the cops! She's going to kill me!"

Sam smiled with a slow twist of her mouth that never quite reached her eyes. "Cops are already here, blondie. According to our neighbor Frankie, who's run off to fetch them for me, they've just gone to get some coffee. But I think you're definitely going to want to talk to them."

"Sam, what's going on?" Jerri asked, while shoving Deuce closer to Sam's side, imploring him with her eyes to do something—fast.

He shrugged his wide shoulders and looked to his brother. "Four?"

A slow, humorless smile spread across Kar'four's mouth. "Sam and I were…talking, here in front of the booth, waiting for you two to catch up, when this woman walked up to us. She made a comment that Sam didn't appreciate. The rest is self-explanatory," he ended with a hard grin.

Deuce snorted under his breath. "Four, that story has more holes than a Synnie's chassis."

Four smirked and opened his mouth to respond but it was Sam's voice that answered. "What he *isn't* saying is that we were in the middle of a heated…*discussion*, when this bitch came up, wearing one of our dusters, which she didn't buy. She asked Four what he was doing with an 'ugly little cow' like me. I decided she could use a short lesson in manners. Those portable clothes racks come apart real quick. This piece of plastic is a bit lighter than a *bō* staff but it's doing the trick."

"That about sums it up," Four agreed, grinning at Sam.

"You're not being much help," Jerri huffed, glaring at Kar'four.

"Who needs help?" he asked, arching one dark brow. "Sam's handling herself beautifully. I'm nearly drooling just watching her in action, waiting for *my* chance to handle her."

Sam's cheeks flushed with crimson color but she kept her eyes on the blonde at the other end of the black plastic rod.

"Yeah…well," Deuce muttered, "you're going to have a hell of a time trying to fuck her if the police arrest her for assault."

Four's expression went hard with anger, the muscles in his shoulders and arms bunching with tension. "It's a hell of a lot more than fucking that I want from her."

"Boys," Jerri murmured, suddenly aware of the crowd they were drawing and the intimate nature of their conversation, "we have an audience."

Both men flushed then nodded, looking back to Sam and the sniveling blonde.

"You're all crazy," the woman blubbered. "Fucking insane! I'm a VIP, for god's sake. You can't treat me like this."

Sam smiled down at her. "VIP or not, hot stuff, you're going to be the first one I suggest when the cops ask if we know who might have trashed our booth and made off with our merchandise."

The woman's eyes narrowed to hateful slits. "You've got to be kidding."

"Do I look like I'm kidding?" Sam asked in a silky slide of words and Jerri groaned under her breath. In a blur of movement, Sam had twisted the rod in her hands, the long length of black plastic spinning rapidly through her fingers before the opposite end stopped at the exact spot against the blonde's throat, all of it happening before the woman had even drawn her next breath.

"You're scaring the shit out of her, Sam."

"Naw, I'm just screwing with her a bit, Jer. She needs to learn to keep her eyes off another woman's man."

"Great. Now she gets possessive," Four grumbled but his mouth was curling into a wicked grin of satisfaction and Jerri knew it was only a matter of time before he'd stake his claim on Sam for good. The man had eyes for no other woman but the curvy little warrior currently putting the fear of god into the woman on the floor.

"Deuce , please!" Jerri groaned, elbowing him in the side so hard that he jumped. "If you don't do something...then...then...I'm not having sex with you," she hissed, immediately adding, "um...at least until tomorrow."

"You wouldn't," he grunted, cutting her a wounded look of disbelief and outrage. "That's twenty-four fucking hours from now, woman!" he added in a shocked growl.

Jerri's gaze narrowed with deliberate purpose. "I didn't say that I'd like it, damn it. But I'll do it if I have to."

Deuce sighed. "As much as I know she deserves it, I think I better take that," he said, stepping forward. In a move that could barely be seen by the naked eye, he'd removed the plastic staff from Sam's grip and snapped it over his knee before she could even make a grab for it.

For a moment Sam simply stared at the blonde as she scrambled to her feet and began backing slowly away. Sam muttered a soft, gritty string of swear words as the woman disappeared into the crowd, then turned toward Deuce. The clear green of her eyes burned with a wild, primitive fire as she stared at the broken lengths of jagged plastic in his hands. "I had plans for that," she snarled in a soft, quiet rasp of sound.

"I'll just bet you did," he snickered, tossing the broken plastic to the side, "but that lady's already got a stick up her ass. One more would be overkill."

Sam glared at him a moment more, then the corner of her mouth twitched, once…then twice, until her shoulders finally began to shake and she began a deep belly laugh that had tears streaming out the corners of her eyes.

"It isn't funny, Sam," Jerri muttered. "You scared me half to death, thinking you were going to maim her or something."

"I'm sorry," Sam laughed, wheezing, holding her sides as her laughter grew. "God, Jer, if you could have seen the look on your face," she giggled, not stopping until Four had grabbed her up in his powerful arms, crushed her against his chest and claimed her with a possessive kiss, taking all of that wonderful laughter into his mouth, filling her with his tongue, clearly savoring her like the sweetest nectar.

Sam groaned in response.

Four growled into her mouth, clutching his hands around her backside, lifting her higher against his body.

Her legs wrapped around his waist while his hands kneaded her ass and Jerri and Deuce shared a meaningful smile.

Without a doubt, the man was staking his claim.

Chapter Six
The Lucky Bastards Have It Made

ഌ

After filing their report with the police, the two couples were finally free to head back to their rooms.

Deuce and Jerri followed Four and Sam as they took an escalator upstairs to the main level and made their way through the crowds toward the elevators. As they crossed the casino, Deuce pulled Jerri aside, his eyes narrowed on a huge wall. A three-dimensional image was projected on the smooth surface, giving the fascinating impression that a baseball game was being played in a huge green field opening off of the casino. Players in pinstriped uniforms raced for the dugouts as numbers flashed in the air above their heads.

The numbers indicated the final score of the game. Cubs seven. White Sox one.

Deuce gave the woman at his side a smug, meaningful smile.

"Yeah. Yeah. You're from the future," Jerri grumbled, a wry curve on her lips. "We should have bet."

His smile turned stern. "That's not what you said earlier." With a hand on her elbow, he steered her toward the elevator tower in the center of the building.

"That was before I lost my entire investment," Jerri complained mournfully. "They took everything! Now that we're wiped out, I'm not feeling so noble."

When they reached the banks of elevators, Sam and Four were nowhere to be seen. Jerri and Deuce stepped into an empty car just as its doors were closing.

"I hope Sam's all right," she said as Deuce gave her a hot, intent stare and closed in on her like an animal stalking its prey. She shivered in reaction, even as she worried about Sam.

His lips skimmed behind her ear and his breath was humid on the sensitive column of her throat. "Why wouldn't she be?" he asked slowly and there was no mistaking the slight catch to his voice, a velvet roughness that revealed his hunger.

Jerri moaned as his warm tongue flicked out to tease the hollow of her ear, her hands grasping onto his round biceps before she melted on the spot. "I just wish she'd…quit fighting it and let go," she said a bit breathlessly.

"You said earlier that she was afraid."

Jerri nodded, another moan escaping as his hands drifted up and down her sides, never quite reaching the swell of her breasts but coming closer with each provocative pass. All around her the glitz and glamour of New Las Vegas attempted its visual assault against her senses, from the mirrored walls of the elevator to the luxurious carpet beneath her feet, yet those distractions faded to nothing and Jerri was conscious only of the hot, hard male body surrounding her, crowding her, making her feel alive in a way that she had never known before. It was as if she had a new awareness of her innate ability to taste, to feel, to take pleasure from the simple act of touching.

It was overwhelming, decadent in the extreme and utterly addictive.

She loved it.

"What is she afraid of?" he prompted, after a moment, when it became obvious she was lost in the sensual touch of his lips against the curve of her cheek, her temple, the corner of her eye.

Jerri struggled for thought, then shrugged. "I don't know, exactly. Falling too far. Falling too fast."

When Deuce nudged his lips behind her ear again, then gently nipped her lobe, she felt a pleasant heat settle below her belly.

"She was in love once before," Jerri began to explain, marveling at how comfortable she found herself with this man. "It was years ago. The guy wasn't the most handsome man on the face of the earth." Jerri shook her head at the memory. "Sam always sold herself short. She thought she'd be safe with someone like Brad. She thought someone like that would appreciate her."

Deuce nodded slightly, his rugged lips grazing her tender flesh, each touch sending a wave of chills cascading over the surface of her skin, while that evocative warmth spilled deeper into her core, melting between her legs like sweet, succulent honey.

"And?" he prompted again, when her words trailed off, the soft, husky rhythm of their breathing the only sound within the smoothly ascending elevator.

"And, he didn't," she added dully. "Sam overheard one of his conversations. He'd been talking to her on his earset and neglected to deactivate the phone when he finished. He was driving in his car with one of his buddies at the time. Talking to his friend. Brad's phone was still on and he was discussing his upcoming wedding…to someone else."

Deuce went completely still, his mouth pressed against her left temple, then slowly pulled away, his eyes swirling with dark emotion as he stared down at her, his jaw hard with shocked, angry tension.

"And that wasn't the worst of it. Brad's friend asked him why he bothered with Sam when his fiancé was such a knockout. Sam heard his answer." Jerri swallowed hard. "Brad said—the *fucking bastard* said—that his beautiful little fiancé wouldn't let him do the things that Sam would let him do to her. His pretty little wife-to-be wouldn't—"

"Don't." Deuce stopped her with a word, cupping her face in his wonderfully warm, capable hands before leaning down and gently pressing his lips against her trembling mouth in a sweetly fleeting kiss that felt like tenderness. Like caring. He drew in a sharp breath, blinking as he pulled Jerri into the broad width of his chest. "I had no idea," he rasped in a whisper. "I had no idea it would be like that in your world. So cold. I assumed that the men of your time treasured their women." He made a rough sound of disgust in his throat, all male anger and anguish, while his expression turned infinitely sad, the deep, mysterious blue of his eyes churning with a wealth of emotion. "The lucky bastards have it made. And they don't even know it. I'm sorry," he said in a low voice. "I'm so fucking sorry, sweetheart."

Jerri swallowed against the tight knot of emotion threatening to choke her and tried for a light laugh. "It isn't your fault."

He shook his head. "I'm still sorry. I'm sorry for Sam and I'm sorry for my brother. Four needs her. Just as I need you. I hope she took a stick to the ungracious bastard," he growled with dark emphasis.

"I wish she had," Jerri agreed just as darkly.

They lost themselves for a moment in the intensity of the other's gaze, while the elevator continued its smooth ascent and then suddenly his long, lean body was pressed up against her, stiff and taut, every line of his hard physique screaming hunger and need. "What floor are we on?" he asked in a strained voice.

Her gaze flicked to the wall. "Eighty-four," she answered in a breathy whisper. "Eighty-five."

"Jerri," he moaned raggedly, his voice heavy with dark, explosive desire. "Could I just...get inside you for a minute? Just to know what it feels like? I feel so damn...cold inside." He took a deep breath that shuddered past his lips and she felt the answering tremor move through his hard, powerful muscles, shaking him against her. "I need your warmth. I won't try to...to finish inside you. I just want your heat surrounding me."

Jerri smiled softly. "Aw," she murmured, "what sort of woman could resist a request like that?" She cast a quick frown at the numbers changing on the elevator wall. "But we'd better be quick. Only sixty floors to go." Nimbly, she worked her buttons loose and shoved her jeans down past her hips, then her knees, until they pooled at her ankles.

With her fingers fumbling from the flash fire of need he so easily created, she struggled to help Deuce with the unfamiliar buttons, nearly groaning when finally he guided his rigid cock out of his jeans.

Bending his knees slightly, his muscles trembling, skin hot and damp, he grasped his broad root and fed his heavy length between her legs, probing for her soft opening and keying into it with his dark, bulging cock head. Taking an unsteady breath, he straightened his legs and entered her in slow, salacious inches. His forehead was warm and damp against hers and his breath came in short, humid bursts. As the thickness of his cock stretched her wide, he gazed intently into her eyes, his expression both beseeching and demanding. She knew he was making a supreme effort not to hurt her but her body was too tight, despite the slick cream of her arousal, and his own need too overwhelming. Still, he struggled to hold himself in check, until she gave him what he needed.

"Deuce, it's okay," she said huskily, bringing her hands up to his face, the burning heat of his skin vibrant against her palms. She cupped the hard line of his jaw, stroking her thumbs against the tense corners of his beautiful mouth, his eyes burning down at her like twin spots of blue flame, brilliant and alive. "I want you. Give me all of you. Please."

A harsh, animal sound broke free of his chest, his strong hands biting into the giving flesh of her bottom and with a final, impaling jerk of his hips, he drove himself into her and slammed up against her limit. His eyes closed a moment in pure, painful ecstasy and she watched as the brilliance of the moment washed over him, through him…and through her as well. Then his lashes slowly lifted, the blue of his eyes dark with hunger and lust and unbearable pleasure and his heavy gaze slid to her mouth.

"Thank you," he said against her lips, moving against her, the feel of his cock like an immense, solid shaft of steel as it pressed even deeper inside her. "Gods, Jerri, *thank you.*"

Then he covered her mouth with his.

* * * * *

While Deuce put a long, tender kiss into Jerri's mouth, the elevator car glided silently upward. One car over, in the adjacent elevator shaft, his brother struggled for control. Like his twin, Kar'four was balls deep inside his chosen woman. Unlike his brother, Four's hips were moving with a blatantly aggressive rhythm as he pinned Sam to the elevator's mirrored wall and drove into her. Around him, the elevator car's environment was sterile and cold, all metal and mirrors but in his arms lived the warmth and passion he'd always craved. His need and hunger for her were like a huge, burning ball in his gut, turning him inside out and he couldn't control it.

Four held Sam's face in both hands as he sucked in a tortured breath. The liquid heat of her sheath pulled an instinctive response from his body, demanded the hard thrust of his cock and he fought the urge to nail her to the wall with a primitive violence that he didn't understand.

"Sam," he groaned, thrusting into her in thick surges of unsettled lust, loving the way her body fought to take him. The intensity of the feeling was so savage that it all but scared the hell out of him. "I wanted to do this slowly," he muttered in a rough, shaky voice. "I *wanted* to feel you orgasm around me before I came. But right now all I want to do is fuck you…fuck you hard…and…and crush you beneath my body." He stopped, panting, searching her eyes. "Is that normal? Mother of Darkness, Sam, I don't want you to think I'm an animal."

"But you *are* an animal," she answered in a lust-laden murmur. "A very male animal with primitive urges and needs. Everything you're feeling is entirely natural, Four."

He nipped at her ear, dragging the small pillow of her earlobe through his teeth. "All right," he rasped, "but don't be surprised if I start growling or…chewing on your neck." At this, he halted, packed up thick and hard inside her clenching body but unmoving. A deep frown creased the tanned skin between his brows. "Why the hell would I want to chew on your neck?"

Sam laughed warmly, running her palms over the hard breadth of his shoulders, loving his size and the steel-edged power she could feel pulsing through his warrior's body. But most of all, she loved the feel of him *there*, buried deep within her, his cock massive and burning in its heat, until she knew nothing but that stinging pressure and fullness. "I'm not sure," she murmured soothingly. "Maybe because you want to mark me. Mark me for other men to see. So they'll know…"

Sam frowned uncertainly as she grappled with the idea. In infinitesimal degrees, her expression changed. A tiny look of revelation was followed by a spark of hope and finally tender warmth as she gazed into Four's eyes. "You're *marking* me," she whispered.

Four nodded slowly, lost in the loving warmth and passion that flooded her green gaze. "So other men will know you're mine." His voice came hard and rough, thick with hunger and primitive possession. "So they'll stay away from you."

Sam reached up with one hand and cleared her sliding wash of honey-brown hair from her neck. "Have at it," she murmured with a husky giggle, then gasped as Four pulled slightly back and then nailed her with an especially vicious thrust just before his mouth opened on her neck. His teeth grazed the tender column of her throat while his hips kept shoving, trying to cram his cock deeper, until he was grinding against the ripe swell of her clit and jerking low, throaty little sounds from her chest.

"I wanted to go slow," he complained harshly as he sucked her flesh into his mouth.

Sam moaned, trembling in his arms. "This is your first time, Four. I want it to be perfect for you. We'll save slow for next time."

Kar'four grunted as he drove against her, slamming her into the wall, undone by the feelings crashing down on him. "But I don't want to do this without you," he growled, hating how needy he sounded but unable to help it. "I want to feel you clench on me. I want to feel your juices gush around me as I go in for the final drive."

Again, Sam moaned, her body pulling on him like a tight, wet fist. "Keep talking like that and I'll be there for you when you say the word."

Kar'four rasped his rough tongue over the pink flush he'd coaxed out onto the surface of her skin. With downcast eyes and a deep sense of satisfaction, he observed his work proudly before dropping his gaze to his groin, where the thick root of his shaft glistened with a sweet wash of Sam's honeyed moisture. "I can't believe I'm here," he whispered. "I can't believe I'm here inside you, watching my cock coated with your juices, stretching you wide, crushing my cock head into the cushion of your womb, feeling your cunt hold me like it owns me." He grabbed her chin and spoke into her mouth as he slammed home and banged her up against the mirror at her back. "If you want to make it perfect," he grated, "come now, Sam."

Like a prayer granted, Kar'four felt her inner muscles flutter twice, then her vagina tightened around his cock and he *saw stars*. Holding his breath, he held perfectly still, savoring the long ripple of her cunt as Sam's sheath contracted the length of his pulsing cock. He shouted her name while she cried out in stunned pleasure. His balls turned to rock and his release jetted through his shaft in blistering surges burning with the stark edge of prolonged satisfaction.

For at least ten seconds after his ejaculation, he rocked against her in short, gentle surges, milking the experience for every last shred of intimate, breathtaking pleasure. They were one, now. Sam was his. Intimately, profoundly *his*. And the way she was holding him, stroking her palm along the damp, rough line of his jaw, told Four she knew it as certainly as he did.

Lost in a haze of sated completion, he panted softly into her mouth as the doors shushed quietly open behind them. Sam's legs were wrapped around his hips beneath the long, dark duster he wore and he stooped quickly to sweep her jeans from the floor of the elevator. With her pants in one hand and his coat tugged around her naked derriere, he carried her out of the car, still impaled on his semi-rigid shaft. "It's all right," he murmured tenderly as she gasped and hid her face against his shoulder. "We're alone."

A low rumble of laugher accompanied the sound of elevator doors opening. "Not anymore, you're not."

Chapter Seven
Sin and Salvation

ဆ

Unlike Kar'four and Sam, Jerri and Deuce weren't attached at the hips as they stepped out of the elevator. But Deuce *did* have a very firm grasp on Jerri's wrist as he towed her down the hall toward their rooms.

After Jerri got the doors open, Four carried Sam across the hotel room and through the interior door to the adjoining room. Quietly, Jerri closed the lovers into the privacy of Sam's room.

For a moment, Jerri stood at the door, watching Deuce.

He returned her stare with so much heat that she felt scorched, his mesmerizing blue gaze electric. "Where were we?" he asked quietly, the corner of his mouth lifting in such a devilishly sexy grin that her toes curled.

Jerri tilted her head, regarding him from beneath the thick fringe of her eyelashes. "Uh. I think you were about to—"

"Fuck you?" he supplied helpfully, the grin melting into a smile so devastating, she was instantly reminded of what he felt like packed up tight inside her, buried deep and hard and thick. That damn elevator ride had been far too short...and far too much of a tease of what she knew was to come.

With her heart all but pounding in her throat, she gave him a sultry nod. "Uh-huh. At least...that's what I was hoping for."

"Hang on, sweetheart," he rasped as he stepped toward her and grabbed her by the hips. "You're about to get more than you hoped for."

Lifting Jerri off the floor, he swung her across the room and pinned her to the bed beneath him, the weight of their bodies sinking them into the plush softness of the duvet. Together they fought her vintage denims down her legs, fingers tangling as they struggled to reveal skin as quickly as possible, their breaths panting a tempo that mirrored the intensity of the need gripping them. The second the jeans cleared her toes, Jerri went to work on her panties, while Deuce stood long enough to get rid of his duster and pants.

Jerri was working on the buttons of her blouse when he climbed back onto the bed, naked and hard and impossibly gorgeous and pushed her knees apart with his. With rough impatience, he shoved the bottom of her blouse up over her breasts. After that, he went crazy for a while, trying to find a way into her bra. "Jerri," he panted, falling back on his heels, "what the fuck is this thing?"

Jerri giggled. "It's called a bra, short for brassiere."

"You weren't wearing one earlier," he complained. "Is it…is it absolutely necessary?"

"In my case it sort of is," she explained, loving the way he looked kneeling there between her spread thighs. "Depending on what I'm wearing."

He leaned over her and hungrily ran his tongue inside the top edge of the lacy fabric that cupped her breasts. His cock made a warm, thick line where it lay against her belly, his hands clenched tightly against the smooth skin of her hips. "What is its function, exactly?"

Jerri thought about this for a while, trying to formulate her answer in such a way that Deuce wouldn't forbid her the future use of her bra. "Um, it stops other men from staring at my nipples," she finally told him, giggling again.

Instantly, he stopped trying to work his tongue inside the lacy cup of the bra. "You're shitting me," he growled.

Jerri laughed at the purely male disgruntlement in his expression, like a little boy who'd just been told he'd never grow up strong and tall unless he ate his broccoli. "Well, maybe a tiny bit."

"*Well,*" he drawled darkly, "you've got about three seconds to get rid of it. After that I take my teeth to it. And when I'm done, all that will be left of your *brassiere* is *maybe a tiny bit.*"

"All right," Jerri laughed. "All right. Jeez, Deuce you're such an animal!"

She felt his weight stiffen above her. Without actually moving, he pulled away from her.

"Deuce? Is something wrong?"

Guilt shadowed his gaze as he stared down at her. He shook his head. Then shook it again. "I'm not an animal," he said, a strange amount of emotion weighting his words.

Again, Jerri took a moment to consider her response. Somehow she knew that what she said next was critical to their relationship. "Are you certain?" she murmured. "Because I thought I detected a dash of the predatory beneath that handsome, sophisticated exterior of yours. And I thought it was incredibly sexy."

It must have been the right thing to say, because his lips curled, his blue eyes flamed and the warm tip of his cock pressed purposefully against the swollen, damp opening of her pussy.

"Yes," she hissed. The emptiness inside her was painful and huge and she was desperate for him to fill it. "Oh god, Deuce, please," she moaned urgently and before the last syllable left her lips, he was driving forward, working himself back into her tightness with short, grinding strokes, filling her up until her clenching body was throbbing around the hard, thick, heated length of his cock. It was beautiful and wrenching, the emotion that crashed through her at that moment, and she cried out softly, arching beneath him.

"I can't hold it anymore," he groaned thickly, lowering his face into the warm hollow made by her neck and shoulder.

"Damn, sweetheart, I want it to last forever but I've got to come."

"It's okay," she panted, his hard, heavy strokes pushing her closer and closer to her own devastating meltdown. "Just...lift my legs, Deuce." The words came out gritty and hoarse but he understood. Scooping her knees over his elbows, he loomed over her, staring wildly into her hazy eyes, their noses nearly touching and drove every massive inch of his rigid shaft into her at a deeper angle, slamming into the tightly knotted pressure of her clit. Jerri screamed, jerking beneath him, the pleasure spiking through her so sharp that it burned directly on the fragile precipice between ecstasy and pain.

"More?" he growled, pulling back, almost leaving her, the ruggedly handsome lines of his face etched with fierce possessiveness and masculine, predatory hunger.

"More," she cried out, "God, yes. All of it."

A hard shiver shook Deuce down to his bones and he growled, "You're going to fucking come with me, Jerri. Do you understand me?"

She went wild beneath him at the provocative command, screaming and shouting and driving him to such intensity that she knew he feared he was hurting her with the savage powering of his body into hers that he couldn't control. But she was clutching at him, drawing him closer, reassuring him with the press of her mouth against his upper lip, the gentle nip of her teeth on his lower one.

And he exploded, dragging her with him as they fell together into the infinite, shattering darkness. The thick, scalding wash of his cum shot into her as her body clutched greedily at his pulsing cock, the spasms so powerful that he grunted with each one. The pleasure rolled on and on, drowning them in sensations too keen to be borne...too powerful not to crave.

By the time she finally lifted her heavy lids, Jerri had no idea how much time had passed. But Deuce was still with her—still *within* her—staring intently into her eyes, his expression filled with wonder and amazingly enough…hunger.

"After two trips into the starting block, it's about damn time we got to finish the race," she murmured softly, her voice sleepy with satisfaction.

"I don't want to pull out of you," he said thickly, carefully releasing her legs, then immediately planting his powerful forearms on either side of her face. "It feels too good."

Wrapping her arms around his wide, slick shoulders, she pulled him closer and held him tightly. "Then stay right where you are."

He pressed a quick kiss to the side of her throat then lifted his head, studying her and she smiled at the look she saw burning there in that provocative, smoking gaze. And just like that, he began growing rigid again. "Damn, Jerri, I…uh…" he trailed off, swallowing hard, his dark skin gleaming and warm, all male animal and passion.

"What?" she asked dreamily, knowing she looked like a lovesick little fool. Her hand moved to his head, fingers sifting through the long, silken strands of his hair, petting him…comforting him.

"I don't know," he began carefully, those hypnotic blue eyes moving over each flushed feature, until she felt as if he were memorizing her, the exact way she looked at this precise moment. "I don't know how to put into words what this meant to me," he finished gruffly. "What this *means* to me."

Something sweet and fragile broke open deep inside her—something she knew and accepted could never be bottled up and hidden away again. "Sam has always accused me of being a hopeless romantic," she said, her voice breathless, "but I need…I need to tell you something."

"What, sweetheart?" His smile was tender and infinitely beautiful.

"I've never…I mean, what happened between us…" she paused, wetting her lower lip with the tip of her tongue, before explaining, "It's never been like that for me before, Deuce."

Instead of withdrawing, both physically and mentally, the way she figured most men would have, he pressed deeper, hitting the mouth of her womb while a very male look entered those powerful blue eyes. A husky, whiskey-rough, "I know," slipped from his lips, a touch of triumph burning bright and warm in his deep blue gaze.

Her brow drew into a frown. "How do you know?"

Another smile—this one all arrogant, alpha male. "I might have been inexperienced when it came to sex with a real woman—a warm, beautiful, *blow-my-fucking-mind* kind of woman," he explained, pressing tender, rubbing kisses against her swollen mouth between each huskily rumbled word, "but I'm intelligent enough to recognize when something is—"

He broke off, searching for the right words and she murmured, "Yeah it was."

"I'm glad," he admitted, staring into her eyes with such raw need and hunger that she shivered from the inside out. "I'm glad that you've never felt that with anyone but me, Jerri."

The smile started deep, blooming from that sweet, fragile spot and with her heart in her eyes, she whispered, "So am I."

* * * * *

Four groaned. It was a long, satisfied sound. "I have a feeling I'm going to be hard for the rest of my life."

He was splayed out on the rumpled white sheets, his dark wash of midnight hair fanning out on the pillow beneath his head, Sam's flushed face resting on his biceps. The sheets bore the intoxicating scent of their lust and passion, rich with sex— something too primitive and beautiful to be bottled.

Reaching across his body, Kar'four took Sam's hand and drew the heel of her palm over his hard, flat abdomen. His eyes were downcast as he watched her smaller hand in his. "I'm never leaving this room, or this bed, again," he murmured in a low rumble, drawing in a long contented breath and letting it out on a deep sigh.

Sam giggled. She turned and snuggled her nose into the soft hair curling beneath his arm, drawing in a lungful of his earthy, masculine scent. "That's all right with me but aren't you going to get hungry?"

Almost on cue, his stomach vibrated beneath her hand as a short growl of complaint issued from beneath the thick stretch of his cock.

Sam giggled again. "I think we'd better feed you guys."

He rolled on top of her, staring down into a pair of sated green eyes that never failed to take his breath away. "Right now, I can assure you, woman, that food is the last thing on my mind."

"Yeah?" she laughed as another deep growling rumble hit their ears. "Well, it sounds like your stomach has a mind of its own. Come on, handsome. We need to keep your strength up."

"There's nothing wrong with my strength," he murmured, smiling crookedly, grinding the long ridge of his damp shaft into her belly.

"That huge hungry beast you're grinding into my tummy is *not* your strength," she informed him. "Your feet are freezing. I think you could use a hot meal as well as some shoes and socks."

Kar'four's eyes narrowed. He wasn't quite content with the way Sam tucked her passion away whenever she found it convenient. "I'll go on one condition," he told her.

"What's that?"

He lowered his head and rubbed his mouth over hers. "After we eat dinner, I get to eat you."

Sam's eyes went a warm hazy green before she blinked the look away with a grin. "Kar'four," she said, "*you* are the master of persuasion."

He couldn't keep his hands off her in the shower. She was so smooth and slippery and deliciously round everywhere. His hands followed the bar of soap as she rubbed a bubbly lather onto her skin. He was so entranced by the texture of her silky wet curves beneath his palms that he completely neglected to wash himself. He continued to caress every naked inch of her body while she soaped him up, leaving his cock for last. By the time she turned her attention to his throbbing hard-on, he was stretched taut and ready to spill. Closing his eyes, he came in the midst of the soaping and the stroking, emptying into her hand as she washed his cock and pulled her fingers over his balls.

After they rinsed off, Sam pushed him out of the bathroom before he could get started again. Rubbing a fluffy white towel over his head, Kar'four left Sam in the steam-filled bathroom, drying her hair. Quietly, he padded barefoot across the plush carpet and eased the door open to the adjoining room that his brother shared with Jerri. As the door inched open, he tilted his head and checked out the room's interior.

Deuce stood before the low dresser, his gaze unfocused on the mirror as he fumbled with the metal buttons on his jeans.

After performing a quick search of the room, Four opened the door wider. Apparently Jerri was still in the bathroom. "Hey," he greeted his brother quietly.

Deuce turned. Like the gleaming surface of gunmetal, his eyes glinted a vibrant metallic blue. "Hey," he answered into the charged silence.

Kar'four stepped into the room, watching his brother keenly. "Did you get any?"

Deuce nodded slowly as the room's golden light played over the mask that hid the upper left side of his face. "Yeah."

Rubbing the hard line of his knuckles over his jaw, Four asked, "Was it amazing?"

Again Deuce nodded. He held his brother's gaze. "She came as I did."

Kar'four expelled a long, slow breath. "I know what you mean," he said in a dark murmur. His blue gaze sharpened with interest. "Did you get to taste her?"

A slow, wicked smile curled across the other man's mouth. "Oh yeah."

"What was it like?"

Deuce's expression was incredulous. "Didn't you get your mouth on Sam?"

"Just tell me what it was like," he grunted.

Deuce taunted him with a mean smile. "Sweetness and sin. Salvation and sensuality. Utter unequivocal heaven." Kar'four groaned while his brother chuckled at his distress. "What the hell were you two doing in there all that time?"

Four blew out a defensive snort. "Rutting like two animals."

"Well, as soon as you get a chance, you gotta get some."

"I will," Four growled. "Although I can't imagine it would be better than Sam's hot, wet mouth wrapped around my dick."

Now it was Deuce's turn to groan as Four slipped him an evil smirk. But his smile dissipated in gradual degrees as he grew thoughtful. "Deuce? Do you think...this is what love feels like?"

His brother lifted one shoulder in a casual gesture, though his expression gave away his inner tension. "I don't know. Maybe. I'm letting Jerri lead the way, here. If she tells me that she's in love then I'm guessing that's what *I'm* feeling."

Kar'four slumped to sit on the edge of the unmade bed. His shoulders drooped a bit. "It's probably too much to hope for but I wish they'd let us know...if they are."

Deuce nodded as he parked his butt on the low dresser. "You don't think we should say something first, do you?"

Kar'four shrugged. "How would I know?"

Deuce snorted. "You read all those damn documents! You should have picked up something."

"As a matter of fact, I picked up a lot!"

"I mean, something besides sex," he muttered.

Four closed his eyes, searching his mind for information. "According to the ancient journals," he recited, "the guy is always the first to tell the girl he loves her."

His brother frowned. "Always?"

"Yeah," Four replied, nodding. "But he doesn't do it until the very end of the story."

"The end of the— *Are you sure?*"

"Positive."

"Well hell." Deuce shook his head slowly. "That doesn't seem very wise."

Kar'four shrugged again. "Who are we to argue with the experts?"

"Okay. We'll have to hold off, then." Deuce pushed out a frustrated sigh. "But it won't be easy."

A clink from the bathroom drew both men's gazes to the closed door. "Get your pants on," Deuce suddenly growled at his brother. "I don't want Jerri walking out here and finding you naked."

Kar'four smirked. "Afraid she might see something she likes?"

He rolled his eyes. "We're identical," he reminded his twin.

"Almost identical," Four corrected him.

Staring at the carpet as if he could find some hidden answer in its luxurious pile, Deuce said, "Completely identical with the masks on."

Kar'four nodded reluctantly. "At least completely identical while we're in…this form."

"Right," Deuce agreed, raising his head.

A thin veil of uncertainty fell across Kar'four's dark features. "Do you think they'll mind? When they find out about us?"

Deuce gave him a stern look. "Of course they won't mind," he said gruffly as his eyes narrowed with defiance. "As far as I'm concerned, it's too late now anyhow. I'll die before I give Jerri up. What about you?"

Four pulled up his chin a decisive notch. "Same here." Then he hesitated, his blue gaze troubled. "I'm just afraid that Sam might be the one who kills me."

Chapter Eight
A Little More Than Ten Seconds

ℬ

When Sam and Jerri were finally ready, the two couples took the elevators downstairs to the convention center and did a little shopping before heading to the roof for dinner. Together, they wandered through the clothing displays. Wordlessly avoiding the aisle that held the remnants of the women's plundered stall, they navigated the packed area until successfully locating several booths offering the latest in men's fashions.

As they moved into the first stall, Jerri pulled Deuce over to a tall rack of men's footwear. "Don't they wear shoes in your time?" she asked, frowning at his bare feet.

He cast a wary look at the offerings. "No."

She eyed him curiously. "But, don't your feet get sore?"

Deuce shook his head as he offered an explanation. "We wear protection on the soles of our feet."

"*Really*?" She stared down at his bare feet, one part of her intrigued by his statement, while the other part—that insatiable, Deuce-addicted new sex fiend she'd discovered living inside her—noted how long and beautifully masculine his feet were. And god, didn't that mean she had it bad, when she started thinking of a guy's feet as beautiful? "What kind of protection?" she asked doubtfully.

Deuce smiled when her gaze lifted to his. "It's hard to explain. Ask me again, later, when we have more time."

"Well, protection or not, you're still going to need shoes. They won't let you into the restaurant without them."

A militant look settled over his gorgeous face, the liquid silver of his mask scrunching as he scowled. Mumbling, "Stupid rules," under his breath, he turned his attention to the available choices.

Waiting patiently as he looked over the various styles, some modern with various straps and synthetic fasteners, mixed in with the older Doc Marten styles and cowboy boots, a niggling sense of unease clouded into the warm rush of sexual, and yes, *emotional,* pleasure buzzing beneath Jerri's skin. On the one hand, she supposed her apprehension was natural, considering the chaotic events of the day but on the other, she couldn't help but think that her anxiety was rooted in a different source. Looking ahead, she worried over what was to come.

Leaving Deuce mulling over the shoes, she moved over to Sam, who stood admiring Kar'four in the footwear she had selected for him—a high pair of black leather boots with a wide turndown just below the knee. After he pulled them on, he frowned down at the dark, soft boots trimmed and edged with silver. "Are you sure these are...current?" he asked. An odd croak of embarrassment in his words made the women share a knowing grin. It was no secret to Jerri that Sam had a wicked pirate fetish—one that the boots were so obviously fulfilling.

"Everybody's wearing pirate boots this year," Sam assured him, winking at Jerri.

"Well if you say so," Four muttered, still staring skeptically at his feet. "But I feel like an idiot, wearing them."

Deuce grinned as he walked over to the group. "That must be why they suit you so well."

Four lifted his hard glare to his grinning brother. "Just wait 'til Jerri picks out your shoes."

That, however, was easier said than done. For some reason, Deuce was averse to the idea of putting anything on his feet. In fact, the girls dragged the men through almost a dozen stalls before he finally settled on a pair of simple slip-on loafers, much to Four's grumbling irritation. Jerri and Sam hid their smiles as Deuce tried them on then tried them out — making certain that he could kick them off easily, shoving the socks Jerri had picked out for him into the deep pocket of his duster.

In the next booth, he looked at several shirts before selecting a soft blue pullover, the color of which complemented his eyes so dramatically that Jerri couldn't have been more pleased. But when it came time to buy a top for Kar'four, there was more trouble. Sam picked out a handsome white shirt with lace cuffs and collar but Four wouldn't even try it on.

"But it's the latest style," she argued, holding the shirt against the front of his body.

Crossing his arms over his chest, he shook his head, refusing to wear anything on his upper body other than the duster he already had on.

"Well," Sam finally grumbled, "you'll just have to button that coat all the way up and *pretend* you're wearing a shirt."

Four gave her a dark, defiant look, holding her gaze as he reached down and fastened one button at about waist level. He looked so determined, not to mention sexy, that Sam must have decided she could afford to compromise. At least, she offered him no further argument.

Of course there wasn't a booth selling men's underwear but by that time Jerri and Sam were tired of arguing with the two stubborn men — tired as well as hungry. They stepped up to the counter, Sam eying her credit key nervously as the clerk waved it at the checkout scanner.

"I'll get dinner," Jerri reassured her.

Unaccustomed to their new footwear, the men kept tripping over their feet on the way back across the casino to the elevator towers. "My feet feel...huge," Kar'four complained as Sam grabbed his arm and steadied him for the third time.

"Thankfully, that's not the only thing that's huge on you," she murmured out the side of her mouth.

He was still laughing when they stepped off the elevator, devilish eyes shining with humor as he and Deuce took off for a quick stop in the men's room.

The women stood together as they waited across the way from the restrooms, in the wide hallway just outside the entrance to the restaurant. Tucking her hair behind one ear, Jerri moved closer to Sam's side, her voice low as she said, "Are you worried?"

"About what?" Sam asked as she turned toward Jerri, propping one shoulder against the wall.

The words tumbled rapidly out of Jerri's mouth, one after another. "About what they see in us? Where this is all going? What's going to happen when they have to deal with this scary robbery shit? What's going to happen after that? What those damn masks are about? Where this is all going?"

"You said that last part twice," Sam pointed out, arching one tawny brow.

"Yeah, well," Jerri muttered, "that's because it's the most important one. Especially…" she paused for a moment, lifting one shoulder before forging ahead. "Especially after this afternoon."

Sam's eyes held a curious fire as she asked, "Was he…um…"

A long, shaky sigh escaped her throat. "Oh yeah."

Sam nodded knowingly. "Kar'four too. I'm surprised I can even walk."

Releasing a deep breath, Jerri leaned back against the wall. "Same for me."

"They *are* out of this world," her best friend pointed out, not exactly sounding happy about the statement.

"Yeah," she mumbled. "That's what worries me."

"I know it's hard and it sucks not to know where this is going," Sam said after a moment, kicking the toe of her shoe against the gleaming hardwood floor, "but I think we're just going to have to go with the flow here, Jer."

"I know, it's just..." She swallowed thickly and stammered, "It's just that I feel really...really attached to him. I don't want...don't want to...to lose him, Sam."

"Then we're just going to have to make certain that we don't lose them. Trust me, I don't want to lose Four either. Not now, when I've finally found him."

Jerri shook her head, deep in thought. "This isn't like us, Sam. What do you think is happening?"

"I don't know. Maybe it's not us. Maybe it's them. They're...they're not like other men."

"You can say that again," Jerri agreed, laughing softly.

"It's like...I don't know," Sam said quietly, struggling to explain. "Like they were *meant* to be here with us." She scrunched her small nose as she slanted a look at Jerri. "Does that make sense?"

"Yeah, that's how I feel. Like no matter how badly I fight it, this is where I'm supposed to be. With Deuce."

The men came out of the bathroom entrance together, side by side, two gorgeous creations of beautiful, rugged masculinity and both women moaned low in their throats then glanced at each other and laughed.

"Oh god, did you see that look?" Sam groaned. "I nearly came on the spot."

Jerri giggled, elbowing her friend in the side. "You're such a perv."

"And you're not?" Sam snorted.

"Well..."

"Hah! You're not fooling me, Burton."

"Oh all right," Jerri giggled. "I admit it, I'm a perv."

"A perv in love," Sam teased her and Jerri felt her face turn bright red, pulsing with the heat of her blush.

Before she could respond, the guys had reached them.

"What'd she just say to you?" Deuce asked, eyeing her blush with heated male interest as he grabbed her with one arm, immediately pulling her into the hard, hot heat of his body.

Staring at his strong, tan throat, Jerri whispered, "Um, nothing."

"I bet I can get it out of you," he teased, lifting her chin with the edge of his fist, those deep blue eyes sparkling with mischief as she met his possessive, playful stare.

"You think so?" She smiled, pressing closer to him, wondering if Sam was right.

Deuce lowered his head, his silken kips finding the sensitive shell of her ear. "When I get it in you, when I bury my cock deep in that delicious little pussy of yours, Jerri, and fuck you hard and deep, like you love it, you'll tell me whatever I want to know."

"Pretty sure of yourself," she responded with a low, shaky laugh, her voice husky and full of hunger…for him. Only for him and the arrogant, grinning ass knew it.

The smile that curved his mouth came slow and wicked and heart-stoppingly sweet. "Hopeful, sweetheart. Just hopeful."

"And what exactly are you hoping for?"

Deuce stared down at her, his thick-lashed blue eyes dark and mysterious. Blinking slowly, he tilted his face to the side as he studied her, both of them trapped in the moment, caught in the web of heat and emotional hunger pulling them deeper and deeper, binding them together. "Why don't we see if you can get the answer to *that* out of *me*?" he finally rasped, his voice a rough, provocative whisper of sound.

With his sexy words came a stunning visual overload of all the kinky, explicitly carnal ways she'd love to do just that.

Oh god, Sam was right! She *was* a perv in love! God, she'd fallen hard and fast and there wasn't a damn thing she could do about it!

Jerri swallowed, her heart all but pounding out of her chest as she licked her lower lip, smiled and said, "Okay. You're on. After dinner tonight, we'll see exactly what I can get out of you."

* * * * *

The rooftop restaurant was open to the dark bowl of the star-freckled sky, while stone pavers underfoot gave the space the ambiance of a sidewalk café. A black, wrought iron railing ran around the perimeter of the tiled rooftop, the heavy metal twisted into artful swirls that merged and divided and merged again. Couples strolled out the length of the elegant barricade, stopping occasionally to lean over the high railing and peer into the city two thousand feet below. A thick, stubby candle glowed on each table, spilling a warm circle of light onto the white lace tablecloths. Silverware clinked against fine, thin china as diners murmured quietly.

Threading their way through the scattered tables, the two couples followed the headwaiter to a cozy table tucked beneath two potted aspens. The leaves rustled and twisted in the dry desert breeze.

Seated beside Sam, Kar'four's hand wrapped around her knee as his contented gaze languished on her face.

"Aren't you going to look at the menu?" she murmured.

He frowned slightly as he glanced at the unopened menu. "It wouldn't mean much to me," he told her. "We don't have anything like this in the future."

A waiter interrupted with a request for their drink orders. After Jerri and Sam ordered, Deuce shrugged. "We'll have what they're having."

"Sir?" The young man's pencil hovered uncertainly over his notepad.

"Drinks. Dinner. The works. Just bring us whatever our women order."

The waiter left the table grinning. When he returned, he balanced four tall, pale blue "ladies specials" on a tray. The slender glasses were garnished with floating pansies and long sparklers spitting little blue stars.

"By the skies, I'm thirsty," Four announced. Reaching for one of the tall, slim glasses, he pinched out the sparkler and upended the drink, emptying it in several long, thirsty swallows. Sam watched, fascinated, as his Adam's apple rode the column of his throat. When the glass was empty, he licked his lips and smiled at her as he returned the glass to the table. "That was great! What was it?"

Sam shot a tiny smile across the table at Jerri. "About ninety percent alcohol," she muttered.

"What's alcohol?" Four queried with an open expression.

Deuce snorted impatiently. "It's a liquid intoxicant that affects your brain. It slows your reflexes and interferes with your ability to reason. Though in your case," he added dryly, "I doubt you'll notice."

"Fuck you," Kar'four answered pleasantly, calling the waiter over to their table and ordering several more of the tall alcoholic beverages.

Deuce arched one dark brow. "Keep drinking those things and you may not be fucking at all tonight, as it can also affect your…er…ability to perform."

Sending a teasing leer in Sam's direction, Four grinned a look of lascivious intent. "Don't worry, sweetheart. When it comes to you, there isn't a force on this planet that could affect my…ability to perform."

Sam rolled her eyes while Jerri giggled and soon after a waitress arrived at the table with four plates. The men dug into their meals almost as soon as the plates touched the lacey white tablecloth.

Deuce took several bites then chewed, his eyes closing in ecstasy. "This is amazing," he moaned. "What do you call it again?"

Jerri shared a wry smile with Sam. "A taco."

He swallowed as he shook his head. "By the seas, we have nothing like this where we come from. Nothing!"

"What is your food like?" Jerri asked.

Deuce shrugged. "You know. It's just food. It's just sustenance. You have to eat it to stay alive. It doesn't taste good or anything."

"It doesn't taste bad," Kar'four interrupted around a mouthful of crunchy corn tortilla.

"No," Deuce agreed. "But it isn't like this. It isn't *anything* like this."

Four grinned at his brother. "You know who'd love this?" he asked, scooping up some of the steaming filling that had fallen out of the taco's crunched shell, the sharp scents of Mexican spices mixing with the dry night air.

Deuce smiled. "Tré."

Sam tilted her head, an interested expression on her face. "Tré?"

"Kar'three," Four explained, "but he insists on going by Tré.

"Kar—" Sam stared at her date. "Another brother?"

Four nodded as his white teeth bit off another mouthful.

"Another twin?" Sam demanded, her green eyes wide with surprise.

Kar'four nodded as he swallowed. "That's right."

"Exactly how many 'twins' do you have?"

Finished with his first taco, Four quickly picked up a second. "Six. There are always six clones to a family."

Jerri looked from one brother to the other. "All identical…" she stated, her face brightening with interest.

Deuce lifted one shoulder in an evasive gesture. "Pretty much. But Tré is the artistic one. He'd…go crazy here."

"So then, your family name is…Kar?"

"That's right," Four answered.

Jerri grinned at Sam. "I can't wait to meet them all."

Deuce's expression turned suddenly solemn. He took a deep breath as Jerri wrapped her hand around his bicep. Looking down at her fingers wrapped around his arm, he closed his hand over hers as he forced a smile onto his lips. "I'm sorry. But if we're successful in stopping the robbery here and averting the plague, our brothers…will cease to exist." He flicked his gaze at Four as the men shared an instant of pain.

Kar'four nodded. "Assuming we're successful here, the future — our future — will have never happened. Our brothers will never have been born. Everything we know will have disappeared the instant we left."

The two brothers settled into a somber melancholy.

Sam caught Jerri's eye, knowing what she was thinking. "What about you?" she asked, carefully broaching the question, unsure as to whether or not she actually wanted to know the answer. "What happens to you after you stop the robbery? Will you…cease to exist?"

Their dates didn't answer right away.

"I mean," Sam persisted, "when the future is changed, *you'll* never have been born either."

"We're not certain," Four answered quietly. "The scientists ran some theoretical equations that looked promising but didn't put the question to a practical test."

"Why not?" Sam sputtered. "You have nothing but time, out there in the future. Why didn't they check? Why didn't you ask? Why didn't you —"

"We didn't ask," Deuce upbraided her quietly. "Everyone we knew was giving up everything — *everything* — to correct the situation. It wouldn't have seemed very gallant of us to ask the question." His blue eyes burned with an incandescent fire as he glared at Sam. "Would it?"

Sam stared at the table, unable to raise her gaze to Jerri's face, knowing damn well what she'd find there and feeling somehow responsible. What had they gotten themselves into?

Kar'four's drinks came in the middle of the heavy silence. Plucking a huge pansy from the colorful concoction, he tucked it behind Sam's ear, inhaled the contents of the first tall, frosty glass in one gulp, then quickly swallowed half of the next one. Rolling the fragile stem of a pansy between his fingers, he threaded the flower into his dark hair then reached across the table for Jerri and Deuce's flowers. When he was done, the starlight glimmered down on the three splashes of color tucked into Four's shining hair, while his mouth assumed a playful grin that was as tipsy as the expression in his eyes.

With her lips pressed together into an unsatisfactory line, Sam scowled at the table while the two men finished off their meals. Although she didn't look at Jerri's face, she could see her friend's plate. And it looked to Sam as though Jerri had lost her appetite just about as thoroughly as she had.

Diners strolled away as the hour got later. A steady hum of traffic rose from the streets below, punctuated now and again by the dull, distant wail of a siren or the whirring rhythm of a helicopter's blades as they roamed above the city, patrolling its streets. Their waiter came and removed the plates after Jerri had waved her credit key at the payment console on the table, his curious gaze landing more than once upon the colorful blooms threaded through Four's dark hair. Oblivious to the young man's grinning glances, Kar'four slouched in his chair, his hand wrapped around an almost empty glass, his quiet attention focused on the woman at his side.

"I think I like alcohol," he sighed in a voice that was slightly slurred.

Sam nodded without looking at him. Instead she fixed her gaze on the waiter who crossed the restaurant and disappeared into the kitchen.

"It takes the hard edges off of things, rounds them off, makes them soft. Soft and round like a beautiful woman. Like Sam." He shifted his gaze to his brother. "What do you think, Kar'two?"

Deuce cleared his throat. "I think if you don't shut up now, you're liable to embarrass yourself."

Kar'four leaned forward, slapping his palm on the surface of the table so sharply that Sam's glass nearly toppled and she had to make a sudden grab for it. "Maybe I don't care if I embarrass myself."

"We talked about this back in the room," Deuce reminded him warningly. "You want to be careful what you say. You don't want to say too much."

"Fuck that," Kar'four growled. "I'm in love," he said, standing suddenly. His chair tipped behind him and crashed against the stone pavers, making the women jump. "I'm in love," he repeated loudly, flinging his arms out to his sides and stumbling away from the table. "I'm in love!" he shouted, spinning slowly in the middle of the deserted rooftop restaurant, his head tilted back to the heavens. A pale blue pansy slid from his hair and floated to the floor while Deuce straightened Four's chair and put it back on its legs. Glaring at his brother, Deuce went after him.

Turning to evade his brother, Kar'four ran and leapt to the top of the railing that enclosed the outdoor restaurant.

Sam stifled a scream, her hand over her mouth as she stared at Four, balanced on the narrow railing, tiptoeing along its length. A soft breeze caught his long duster and it opened like a cape behind him, tugging him off balance. Swiftly, Sam moved toward him.

But not swiftly enough. As Sam watched helplessly, the wind gusted and carried him away.

Kar'four disappeared, plunging toward the street two hundred floors below.

"No!" Sam screamed, throwing herself at the railing.

Jerri and Deuce dragged her away from the building's edge, while her fingers clawed at the metal railing.

"It's all right," Deuce kept insisting. "It's all right, Sam."

All right? How could anything possibly be all right? "No!" she screamed again.

Deuce grabbed her by the shoulders and turned her, giving her a rough shake to get her attention. "Listen to me, Sam! Listen to me. He's not dead."

Sam stopped screaming, grasping at the soft fabric of Deuce's pullover, wanting more than anything to believe him. "He's not dead?" she cried.

He shook his head. "At least," he muttered, "I don't think so." He headed for the elevators, dragging the two women behind him as he growled, "Two hundred stories times ten feet times two divided by the acceleration of gravity. What's the square root of 125?"

"What?" Jerri whispered, her face drawn with shock as she put her arm around Sam's shaking shoulders.

"Never mind. A little more than ten. He had a little more than ten seconds."

"He had a little more than ten seconds to what?"

Deuce pulled the women into the elevator behind him. "He had a little more than ten seconds to get his coat off and get his wings out before he hit the ground."

Chapter Nine
About the Masks

ഔ

The elevator slid to a smooth, silent stop and Sam stumbled through the doors as they parted, rushing straight into a hard male chest. "Oomph," she grunted, planting her hands against the unyielding surface so smooth and warm beneath her hands. Pushing back, she lifted her watery gaze and stared with amazement into the deepest, darkest blue eyes she'd ever seen.

Kar'four.

He was alive and whole, albeit missing his long black duster.

"Oh Jesus, Kar'four," she tried to shout, surprised when her voice came out as little more than a ragged, desperate croak. "Why aren't you dead?"

Kar'four's gaze shifted around the crowded lobby, as his long fingers clenched around her upper arms. "Not here, Sam."

Sam shook her head, unable to believe what she was seeing. Slowly, her hands lifted to his dark face, fingertips moving in featherlight strokes across his silken skin, investigating the beautiful arc of his cheekbone, the masculine blade of his nose, before landing gently against the cool metal of his mask. The touches were shaky, her fingers trembling as her eyes went glassy with emotion. Behind her, Jerri and Deuce watched — Jerri's expression shocked, while Deuce appeared more…worried.

Lifting one large hand to the back of her head, Four's fingers rubbed gently against her skull as he cradled her within his wide palm, his fingers moving against the silken slide of her hair. A fierce, intense look of need tightened the powerful features of his beautiful face, while tenderness softened the corners of his mouth where her thumb brushed gently back and forth. "I'm fine, Sam. Calm down, honey. I'm fine."

"You're fine," she whispered, sounding dazed.

Looking over her head, Four shared a meaningful look with his brother, then jerked his chin toward the open elevator doors. "Let's get out of here."

"You're fine," she repeated, her voice sounding odd, her expression shifting. Suddenly her hands paused and for a moment she held perfectly still. "How can you be fine?" she demanded, a decisive thread cutting the words that had Jerri sending an anxious look in Deuce's direction.

"Four's right, Sam," Jerri murmured gently, though there was an urgency beneath the words that clearly bled through. "Let's all just go back up to our rooms."

"Yeah let's," Sam agreed, while a green fire began to slip through the darkening depths of her gaze. The hands that had moments before explored Four's face with shaky emotion now lifted away, only to land with a hard shove against the immovable strength of his shoulders, slapping loudly against his dark, bare skin. "But first," she muttered, "I want this big idiot to explain. I want him to explain right now, Jerri." A vivid wash of color crept over her face as another sharp smack followed her words. "I want him to tell me exactly what he thought he was doing jumping…off…the…damn… roof!"

"Sam," Four began, seeing the glistening sheen of her tears as they thickened on her long lashes. Shaking his head, his voice gruff with emotion and wonder, he whispered, "Please don't cry, baby."

"Don't you *baby* me," she sniffed, poking him in the center of his chest with one pointed finger. "Are you insane? Suicidal? Trying to—"

"Damn it, I didn't jump," he growled, cutting off what was sure to become a blistering tirade.

"Kar'four, I saw you! You jumped up on that damn railing and you—"

"Tripped!" he cut in with a disgusted note of embarrassment.

"Yeah right," she laughed, the sound mocking, clearly disbelieving.

"I didn't do it on purpose!" Four shouted. Then, with another quick look at their surroundings, he lowered his voice. "I tripped," he said succinctly. "It was those damn fucking boots that *you* insisted I wear!"

Her eyes went wide as her head tilted down, eyes locking on the flamboyant pirate boots. "The boots?"

Grasping her wrists, Four pulled her cold fingers to his mouth. Her gaze lifted and she watched as his lips, so warm and soft, pressed against her skin in a reverent caress. "I know I scared you, sweetheart, but please…let's just go upstairs."

"Fine, I'll give you an elevator ride," she agreed hoarsely. "But then I want an explanation."

"Four," Deuce grunted when his twin nodded his immediate agreement.

Blowing out a hard breath, Four shifted his troubled gaze toward his brother. "She deserves to know."

Deuce took a step forward. "Four, damn it, you're not thinking clearly."

"I'm thinking fine."

"You're drunk!" he growled.

"Not bloody likely," Four snorted. "Falling out of the fucking sky has a way of really clearing a guy's mind, trust me."

"And if they can't handle it?" Deuce demanded, sounding almost…panicked.

"How long can we go on *without* telling them, brother? It's time they know."

"Know what?" Jerri demanded, looking worried. "Handle what? What aren't you telling us?"

Staring up at Four, studying the burning brilliance of his deep blue gaze while the lobby lighting glinted against the silvered metal of his mask, Sam nodded her head in understanding. "They're going to tell us, Jerri."

Watching Deuce as he glared at his brother, Jerri forced the words out of a tight throat. "Tell us what, Sam?"

Turning toward her best friend, Sam struggled with what to say, though she knew Jerri understood what was coming. The other woman couldn't take her dark eyes off the upper half of her lover's face. When Jerri's worried gaze finally broke from Deuce and met her own, she simply said, "About the masks."

Nodding, Jerri's white teeth bit gently into her lower lip. "What about them?"

Taking a deep breath, Sam forced her voice to come clear and hard. "What they should have told us from the beginning, Jerri." Casting a hard look at her lover's dark face, she said, "They're finally going to tell us what they're hiding."

* * * * *

The men were silently somber, saying nothing on the elevator trip to the 160th floor. Deuce's grip crushed Jerri's hand as they walked the corridor to the hotel room door. She could have sworn her partner was dragging his feet as he followed his brother. Once inside Jerri's room, the two men separated, as if squaring off for conflict. Taking Sam's hand, Jerri squeezed her friend's fingers as they sat together on the edge of the bed. Nervously, she smoothed the palm of her other hand over the eyelet duvet on which she sat.

With his hand open, Deuce gestured toward his brother. "Go ahead," he invited Kar'four in tight tones laced with cynicism.

Four lifted his chin, looking suddenly apprehensive. "Where should I start?" he asked his brother.

Deuce arched a critical eyebrow. "What difference does it make? None of it's going to look good. Start with the mask. You'll have a hard time getting it off, afterward."

"Afterward?" Jerri echoed, her uneasy gaze moving between the two men.

Kar'four nodded in answer to Jerri's question but his worried stare was fixed on Sam's face. He cleared his throat. "You know we're clones," he stated then immediately hurried on. "We were cloned from a human male. But after creating the cells containing our human DNA, the scientists needed a place for the cells to grow and develop. Obviously, there were no human females to donate the eggs or carry the embryos." Kar'four hesitated then continued after taking a steadying breath. "The scientists were forced to look to the animal world for host mothers. The human cells were introduced into the eggs of various female mammals. At first, the host animals rejected the embryos. Eventually, scientists learned that they had to make the embryos compatible to the host mothers. They had to include animal DNA along with the human DNA so that the host females wouldn't reject them. Keep in mind, the main objective of the program was to keep man alive so he could continue his work to undo the past. His appearance wasn't the main concern—as long as his brain was fully functional, as long as he had fingers and thumbs and a means of locomotion." Four cleared his throat. "My host mother…could fly," he told the women.

Jerri shook her head as Sam stared at her handsome lover.

"Your mother was a…a…flying mammal?" Sam choked out.

"His mother was a bat," Deuce cut in ruthlessly.

101

"A bat!" Jerri exclaimed. "That's not possible. Bats are tiny."

"My mother was a bat of the genus pteropus. She was a flying black fox with a wingspan of six feet. She only had to carry me for the first five months of my life. After that, I was taken from her to finish my development in an incubator."

Sam's face was pale. "But—"

"Sam," Kar'four pleaded. "Don't interrupt. This is hard enough to get out." Reaching for the top edge of his silvery mask, he peeled the glinting metal away from his face.

Beneath the beautiful flow of silver, Kar'four's upper face was covered with a short coat of glossy black fur. The dark pelt ran along his cheekbone, surrounded his eye and disappeared into his hairline. Kar'four's expression was mournful as he explained, "The fur grew where my face touched my mother's uterine wall."

Nodding dumbly, Sam gazed at Kar'four's face. Finally she said, "But that doesn't explain how you can fly. Deuce said something about wings! And I don't *see* any wings!"

"That's because you haven't seen the worst yet," Deuce snorted. "Transform for the ladies, Kar'four. Show them what you got."

Kar'four cut a sharp glare at his brother as he turned his back to the women. For several seconds he stood with his arms tensed at his sides, his fingers splayed out like stiff claws. Then he threw out his arms. As Jerri watched, his biceps as well as his forearms lengthened and stretched. From his newly elongated limbs sprang leathery flaps. As he turned again to face the women, Jerri stifled a scream of surprise. His arms were gone. In their place were huge, tent-like wings. Where the wings met his shoulders, they matched the color of his flesh. From there on out to their tips, the color of his wings shaded from deep tan to darkest ebony. His fingers had lengthened into four long spines that separated the partitions of his wings. His thumbs were tight curling claws placed midway along his wingspan, hanging at the point at which his wings folded.

He was a monster.

If his wings had sprung from his back, he might have looked like some beautiful winged god. As it was, he looked like some horrific experiment gone wrong. A man trapped between exquisite humanity — male perfection at its best — and something base and beastly. Jerri held her friend's hand tightly, afraid to look at Sam, afraid to witness her reaction. With her lips pressed together into a tight line, Jerri wondered how she, herself, would deal with Deuce's transformation when it was his turn. She was determined to handle it well no matter how repulsive she found him. But Jerri couldn't help the shudder that crept along her spine and lifted the hair on her nape. Bats! Jerri was terrified of bats.

Now she understood her lover's earlier reaction when she'd teasingly called him an animal. The men were ashamed of their animal heritage. They thought it diminished them as humans. Jerri knew intuitively that it was unhealthy for them to reject this side of their nature. In order for them to be at peace with themselves, they needed to embrace their animal side and put their self-doubt behind them.

Nervously, she shot a sideways glance at her best friend.

Sam tilted her head pensively as she gazed at Kar'four standing before her. Slowly, his long, slatted fingers moved together as his wings started to fold in against his sides. His expression was melancholy as he searched Sam's eyes.

"Wait a minute," Sam told him softly as she stood and moved toward him. "I want to know what it feels like to be wrapped up in those arms...wings...arm-wingy things. Can you do that?"

Love flared in Kar'four's eyes. Brilliant blue softened and warmed to deep cobalt. He reached out one long finger and hooked the tip behind Sam's shoulder. His tent-like wing followed, wrapping around Sam and drawing her inside his rustling embrace.

Chapter Ten
A Leap of Faith

ဢ

As he hugged Sam closer to his body, wrapping her within his extensive wings, Four caught Deuce's troubled, almost aggressive stare. "Your turn, brother," he prodded with a small smile of encouragement, understanding the source of Deuce's hostility...and hoping for his brother's sake that Jerri proved to be as understanding as her best friend.

But the darkness that shadowed Jerri's tense gaze made his stomach knot with dread for his brother.

Deuce's eyes shifted, his questioning gaze searching Jerri's tight expression, the grooves around his mouth deepening with what he found there. "Jerri," he began but she stepped forward, shaking her head.

"No, it's okay, Deuce. I'm ready. And I...I love bats," she lied, pasting a bright smile on her face. "I've always been...um, fascinated by them."

His face fell, disappointment and concern darkening his features. "That's...great," he said thickly, his deep voice scratchy and raw, "but how do you feel about...aquatic mammals?"

For a moment she only blinked at him then her breath whooshed out of her in a joyful sound of relief. Her dark eyes gleamed with blossoming hope. "I love aquatic mammals!" she answered in a burst of enthusiasm.

Deuce eyed her skeptically, knowing that she'd avoid hurting his feelings if she could. Crossing his long arms over the broad width of his chest, he struggled to control the furious, painful pounding of his heart. "But you just said that you love bats."

"I do," she argued, nodding her head, "but I *adore* seals — sea lions, walruses, whales. Especially whales!"

"Yeah?" he challenged her. His eyes narrowed a bit. "Even Orcas? Killer whales? I know humans tend to find them…intimidating."

Her dark, velvet brown eyes went wide then focused more intently on him, a curious gleam burning behind the rich, lustrous brown. "I'm not afraid of them," she said simply, her lips curving just the slightest bit as a smile tucked into the corners of her mouth, softening her expression. "I…I think they're beautiful, Deuce."

"Even killer whales?" he asked again, the skepticism and fear in his voice too obvious to miss, a terrible sense of vulnerability pouring over him that he'd never known before. It was her — this one fragile, delicate woman — who had sent him to this raw, wounded place and Deuce knew that she was the only one who could lift him out of it.

Damn Four and his irritating sense of honesty!

"Of course killer whales," she said, her voice stronger as she took another step in his direction, that soft, warm scent of her skin reaching his nose, bringing his enhanced senses to life. "I mean, they're beautiful…intelligent. Powerful. What's not to like about them? What's not to love?"

He rolled his shoulders, trying to relieve the cramping in his muscles, everything feeling heavy and thick within his tension-tied body.

"Deuce," Four rumbled, "just show her. It's going to be okay."

Staring at his feet, unable to meet that glowing look of promise in her eyes, he grated the words from a dry, constricted throat. "Just promise you won't scream, Jerri."

"Deuce," she sighed and suddenly her soft, satin palm was cupping his cheek, tipping his face to meet the tender expression that graced her features. "Whatever you're afraid of, it's not going to make a difference."

"You can't know that, Jerri," he argued, his voice tight, the words forced out through his clenched teeth. "You can't know that until you see what we had to become in order to survive."

Her dark brows rose in challenge. "Well, I didn't go screaming at the sight of bat boy over there, did I?"

He grimaced. "You said you *loved* bats."

"Yeah and I lied, in case it escaped your notice." Leaning closer, she lowered her tone to a conspiratorial whisper. "Don't tell your brother but bats scare the hell out of me."

Off to their side, Kar'four laughed softly, nuzzling Sam's throat until she was moaning in his embrace, clearly at peace with his animal side. Deuce couldn't help but wonder if he would find the same acceptance in Jerri's arms. By the seas, he didn't want to do this!

"I don't want to scare you," he rasped, his features tightening with dread.

"You don't," she promised, her smile widening, making his breath catch. "Now strip that mask off and show me, Deuce. Show me everything."

He breathed deeply through his nose, hyperaware of his pounding heart, until it seemed the throbbing rhythm filled his head, the room echoing his fears in a loud, crass display that made him want to cringe with embarrassment. "I will, Jerri. Just...why don't we —"

"Now, Deuce."

He scowled at the commanding tone of her voice, as well as the mutinous expression settling between her smooth, dark brows. "Gods, you're pushy, woman."

"I know I reacted like a scared little ninny a minute ago but it just took me a moment to sort it all out in my head," she explained in a fervent voice, her hand still cupping his check. "Even if you were a bat, I'd...I'd have still felt the way...the way I feel about you. I know you would never hurt me and I know you're the most beautiful thing I've ever seen. All parts of you, even the ones you keep hidden."

He snorted a sharp blast of sound. "That's easy for you to say before you've seen them, Jerri."

A sound of frustration rumbled in the back of her throat, her smile fading as she stared up at him. "Deuce, no matter what's under there, you're still *you*. Still the man who has made my head spin for the past…oh my god…"

"What?" he demanded, grasping her waist. "What's wrong?"

She shook her head in wonder, a misty look of surprise washing over her delicate features. "It's just…I've not even known you for an entire day yet and it feels like…"

"More," he offered in a husky whisper, understanding exactly what she meant.

"Yeah, like we've squeezed days into a few hours." Running her fingers over the glinting metallic surface of his mask, she sent him a warm, tempting look of promise that damn near made his toes curl. "Why don't we see what we can squeeze into a whole night?"

Lowering his voice, he pulled her closer, growling, "I'd rather see what we can squeeze into you."

"You mean something like you?" she laughed, teasing him, dark eyes shining with an intoxicating playfulness that made him want to trap her against his body and never let her go.

"Yeah," he murmured, pulling her hips against his thickening erection. "That's exactly what I mean."

She nudged against him, the look in her eyes burning bright and daring. "I'm game, Deuce. But first, we're going to get this pesky little problem out of the way."

"But you—" he swallowed tightly, wishing they could just go back to where they were, before Four had to go and fall off the fucking roof. "You might not want that anymore."

You might not want me.

"Have more faith in me, Deuce." Her voice was soft and sweet, the touch of her hand sliding through the hair at his temple even sweeter. "It took a leap of faith for me to believe your story, the way you've landed in my life…the things that will soon happen, the changes that we're going to help you fight for. Now it's your turn to take that leap."

For the first time in his entire adult life, Deuce felt like throwing a tantrum. "I'd rather just fuck you," he muttered, knowing he sounded like a petulant child.

Her eyes narrowed. "And that's not happening until you stop being such a dolt and just trust me!"

"Damn it, why go messing with something that's so fucking good, Jerri?" His hands tightened, shaking her slightly. "Why are we pushing it when we could just—"

"Time's up," she growled and with a sudden movement that caught him off guard, she grasped the lip of his mask. The sensitive skin under its edge tingled as her fingers slipped beneath the malleable rim, ripping a groan from deep in his chest.

For a moment, her fingers stilled. "Am I hurting you?" she asked, her voice gentle and soothing, filled with concern.

"No," he growled, his cock thickening some more, making an unmistakable bulge in his jeans that she couldn't miss…and didn't.

With a sly, siren smile, she leaned closer, lifting up onto her tiptoes so that she could press the damp heat of her mouth against his as she pulled the mask completely away, letting it drop to the thick carpet beneath their feet. "I think you like being touched here, Deuce," she whispered, running her fingertips over the smooth, black whale skin that she'd revealed.

"My skin is…highly receptive to stimulus," he gasped, tremors of sensation racking his body as she touched him— learned him—sending a knowing ache for her burning through his blood that nearly brought him to his knees. In a voice graveled by need, he tried to explain. "Whales absorb information about their surroundings through the surface of their skin." He swallowed hard. "It's so damn sensitive."

"It's beautiful too," she whispered, the smile blooming across her silken lips making something in the vicinity of his heart give a sudden lurch, like an internal earthquake that shook him to the core. "Show me the rest now," she murmured, her smile warm and womanly. "It's okay. Let go."

A long, powerful quiver rode the rigid line of his body as he took a step away from her. Without taking his eyes from hers, he kicked off his shoes and allowed the changes to overtake him.

Her eyes held his dark, burning stare as his upper body transformed in a strange testament of man's desperate attempt to match god's work. His neck, shoulders and biceps thickened with the burly strength of a long-distance swimmer while his chest deepened around his expanding lungs. When he turned slightly to the side, Jerri's eyes widened at the shallow black fin that formed a long, rippling line from the base of his skull all the way down to his tailbone. She eyed the strange black dorsal then lowered those soft brown eyes down his body, not stopping until she reached his feet. His toes had elongated, fanning out into long, webbed fins.

The seconds ticked by forever, stretching out slow and torturous, until she finally lifted her gaze, locking her eyes with his. "Do you know what I think?" she asked softly, her voice husky with emotion.

Swallowing the lump in his throat, Deuce shook his head. "What?"

Her small, pink tongue flicked against her lower lip, making him groan. "I think that after I have my wicked way with you tonight…I'm going to have to drag you down to the pool."

He blinked down at her, wondering where this was going and hoping like hell that she was going to keep him together, instead of breaking him into a million shattered pieces. Of course, the outlook was promising…if she was really planning on having her way with him. A spark of hope caught fire in his gut, warming him from the inside out. "The pool?" he rumbled, the small smile playing at the corner of his mouth feeling shaky and uncertain.

"Yeah," she whispered, taking a step closer before reaching up to thread her fingers through the hair at his temples, then drawing his face down to hers, her breath tangling with his as she spoke against his lips. "I've always wanted to have sex in a swimming pool."

"Yeah?" he groaned, his body quaking with eagerness — with hunger. "How about being fucked up against the side of the pool? My breath filling your lungs, my cock driving into your body, taking you so hard that your tender little cunt turns swollen and bruised from the pounding of my body into yours as I force you to keep coming and coming and coming beneath me?"

Jerri moaned into his mouth, her body shivering against his. "You want to know what I'd say to that?"

"What?" he groaned, nipping at her chin, pressing a hard, hungry kiss against her mouth before sinking his tongue deep inside, eating at the sweet, moist well with all the raging, rioting emotion roaring through his system.

"I'd say," she panted, keeping her mouth against his as she shared her sweet, wondrous smile, "that it sounds better than winning the jackpot!"

And with those words, the last of his fear melted away.

Sam smiled when she saw her best friend wrapped in Deuce's tight, meaningful embrace. "They look…happy," she murmured, resting her cheek against Four's steady heartbeat.

"Mmm…I know the feeling."

Her smile widened at the contentment she could hear in his husky words. Contentment, sharpened by that constant need that he carried…for *her*. The same need he'd carried since they'd met earlier that day. "Do you know what it's time for now?" she asked, turning her face up so that she could stare into his beautiful blue eyes.

A sweet, hopeful smile softened the edges of his mouth. "I know what time I want it to be," he growled, his gaze teasing and bright.

Sam gave a soft laugh in return, amazed at the peace she felt at knowing the truth about what he'd been hiding. The only thing marring the perfection of the moment was the fear of what might happen when the robbery was stopped in two day's time and the fate of these two amazing brothers finally decided. But she refused to let that concern ruin her time with him now. No, it was too precious, too priceless not to enjoy to its fullest. Sending him a warm look from beneath her lashes, she whispered, "It's time for you to do something you've never done before."

His grin melted into a slow, sensual smile, eyes lighting with heated interest. "This has definitely been a day for firsts. Time travel. Making love to a beautiful woman. Eating delicious food. Falling off a rooftop. Getting drunk *before* falling off the rooftop," he added wryly, before playfully growling, "Oh…and making love to a beautiful woman."

"You sound like Jerri."

His brows rose. "How so?"

Sam snickered softly. "You said that last one twice."

His slow smile spread into a wolfish expression of hunger, while the look in his eyes flowed into something sharp and predatory. "That's because I'm hoping like hell that I'm about to get lucky. And don't think I don't remember what you promised me for dessert, Sam. Time to spread your sweet little thighs and—"

"Fly," she giggled, sending him a teasing wink as she stroked her fingertips across the top of his right wing where it met his shoulder.

"Yeah," he growled in a low voice, for her ears alone. "I'm starving, Sam. I want to know what my woman tastes like."

She sighed dramatically, mischievously, fully aware that she'd never had so much fun with a lover. "And here I was going to make an innocent comment about how it was time for your first night's sleep in a bed with a woman. A *real* woman."

"Not just a woman. I'm talking about *the* woman. *My woman.* And we can sleep after." Turning his head toward the other couple, he said, "Deuce!"

"Yeah?" his brother mumbled, the words muffled by Jerri's skin as the man pressed kiss after kiss to the side of her throat. A low growl vibrated in Deuce's chest as Sam's best friend stroked her thumb over the smooth black skin covering the upper left side of his face.

"Not to be rude, brother, but get lost."

Pushing the handful of warm, willing woman in his arms back toward the bed, Deuce snickered under his breath. "Actually, Four, this is Jerri's room. *Mine* and Jerri's room."

"Right. Sorry," Four muttered sheepishly, pushing Sam through the connecting doorway. Once the door clicked shut behind them, he pulled her into an eating kiss, his mouth moving over hers in a blatant attempt to get as deep into her as he could. She moaned, undone by the evidence of his need and with a pure, wondrous sound of masculine joy, he swept her up into the cradle of his wings, laughing as he spun her around…and around…and around.

And Sam felt her heart spin crazily out of control.

Dizzy and so hard he wondered how the constrictive jeans managed to hold together, Four lowered Sam to the edge of the bed, then stepped back. Spreading his wings wide at his sides, he took a deep breath then waited as they slowly morphed back into the strong, dark arms of a man.

Sam shook her head from side to side as she stared at him, a misty look in her soft green gaze that melted into him, making him feel shaky and warm, the feeling a million times more potent than that delicious pour of alcohol had been through his system. "You didn't have to do that for me, Four."

"I know," he rasped, his throat feeling tight, "and there's no way to explain what knowing that means to me. But I want to hold you in my arms, Sam. I want to feel my hands on you, touching your skin, making you go crazy beneath me…among other things."

She arched one honey-brown brow. "What other things?"

"Like I said, dinner was delicious—"

"I seem to recall you liking the alcohol too," she cut in with a wry smile.

"Yeah," he laughed, "but…I'm ready for the sweet stuff now, woman. The good stuff. The best."

"Oh?" she murmured, pressing the palm of her hand against his hard abdomen, his muscles jumping under her touch as she stared up at him. "And what are you having?"

"Sweet, sumptuous, succulent Sam," he drawled, grinning like a devil. "And she's a tasty little thing," he growled, pulling her to her feet. He buried his face in the crook of her shoulder, nuzzling her sensitive throat, tickling her with his mouth until she squealed, wriggling against him.

She was panting, laughing and then shrieking as Four lifted her in his arms and tossed her up on the high mound of pillows, where she bounced once atop the ivory eyelet duvet. His hands immediately went to work on his cumbersome jeans as he growled, "Get those fucking clothes off. Now, Sam."

Soft green eyes went heavy, hazy as she watched him pull and tug at his jeans, her own hands moving quickly to undo buttons and slip off her shirt. When she lay in nothing, having shimmied out of her bra and panties, he crawled onto the end of the bed, naked and hard, his cock aching with a thundering, pounding rhythm that matched his heart.

"Open up."

"You don't have to ask me twice," she replied, her smile slow and sexy, eyes bright, cheeks flushed a warm shade of pink as he moved between her spread thighs. He wanted to run his mouth over that blushing pink in her cheeks, take the flavor and scents of her skin into his head, while he lost himself in her.

"Wider," he growled, lowering his gaze to watch her beautiful pink sex open before him, her flesh slippery and blushing with warmth, the smell of her skin and honeyed juices making his head spin. Lifting one shaky hand, he spread the swollen folds farther apart, swallowing a thick lump of lust as he viewed the darker, fiery center of her, her clit a hardened little bud above, while a bit lower the opening of her sweet channel fluttered, glossy and puffy, so tender and fragile looking. Mother of Darkness, he couldn't wait to slip his tongue inside her — right there — and feel those strong inner muscles sucking on him, while he fucked her in a slow, teasing rhythm.

Nothing he had ever read, no matter how hot or provocative or sexually stimulating, compared to having her like this, open and defenseless before him, waiting for whatever he wanted to do to her.

And by the skies, the things he wanted to do to this woman.

Sweet, decadent moments later, Sam's fingers twisted in his sweat-dampened hair, her lush body warm and dewy beneath him, while his mouth moved over her, against her, within her, unable to get enough. His face was wet with her slick, honeyed cream, his mouth flavored with her as he dipped greedily into her gently pulsing channel and fucked her with the long, savoring strokes of his tongue.

"You...you're..." he panted, growling, lips moving against the damp, slick heat of her folds as he tried to get the words out. But his tongue felt thick like his blood, his pulse, his brain, everything weighted down in pleasure at the intimate, carnal beauty of eating her like this, of making a meal of her perfectly delicious little cunt.

"What?" she groaned, her soft voice husky and raw from her harsh cries of pleasure, while she shivered atop the bedding, writhing, her thighs sprawled wide in total abandon, giving him complete access to everything he wanted.

"*You...you're...so...fucking...amazing,*" he growled, meaning every word.

"Amazing enough to stay with?" she asked quietly, staring down at him over the swell of her breasts, nipples tight little knots of need, stomach quivering with each trembling breath. "Forever?"

Kar'four didn't answer her right away. He simply lost himself in her for a little bit longer, letting his lips move over her smooth, silken flesh, so slick and pink and fucking incredible. God, he'd never get enough of her. Of her taste, her scent, the way she melted into his mouth and made him feel like a fucking conqueror because he'd been the man to make her scream and writhe in ecstasy.

It was a bigger high than any victory he'd ever experienced.

Better than anything he could have ever imagined and he'd had so many years to dream...to hunger...to wish.

He raised his head, crawling up her body.

"I give you my word that I'll do everything I can to stay," he grated, his voice harsh and gritty with conviction. "To stay here with you, Sam."

His hands held her head as he balanced on his elbows, all ten fingers threaded through her hair, pressing into her scalp. He stared down at her, eyes hot with desire and the thick rush of emotions consuming him. "How could you possibly think I

116

would leave you? If it's my choice, I know exactly where I'll be."

"Are you sure?" she asked and the hint of vulnerability in her green gaze nearly destroyed him.

"I know where I belong," he rasped, prodding the slick heat of her entrance with the blunt tip of his rigid, aching cock.

He belonged right here, in this time, with this woman who broke his heart with her smiles and made his body, his very soul, ache with the need to have her close.

Four lowered his mouth over the soft silk of her lips, slipped his tongue inside and shared with her the heady taste of her desire. "Take me in, Sam," he groaned. "I'm so cold without you."

Holding his stare, she moved her damp palms over his hard buttocks and began pulling him into her body. "Remember in the elevator, when I called you an animal, Four?"

"Yes," he hissed, lifting himself up on his arms so that he could watch his penetration. Sweat poured into his eyes, hair hanging damp around his face, muscles vibrating as her slick heat coated the heavy head of his cock and the brutal pleasure rolled down his spine, through his legs, until he felt it curl his toes.

"Show me," she whispered in a throaty plea, lifting her hips in a provocative roll that took him deeper, her snug flesh hugging him so tightly, tiny little pulses fluttering through those silken inner walls, stroking the rigid mass of his cock. "Show me again, Kar'four. Take me as hard as you want and show me how much of an animal you can be."

"Oh shit," he groaned, nearly swallowing his tongue as he slammed forward, driving deep, feeding every inch of his shaft into her body in a violent thrust that made her jerk beneath him. Before he pulled back, her hands were gripped in one of his, arms forced up high over her head, stretching her out beneath him, his mouth latched onto one puffy nipple, suckling her hard and strong and fast. His other hand hooked behind her left knee, pulling her leg up high and close to her body, letting him sink deep...then deeper still as he pulled out and drove back in, forcing his thick length into her cunt, muscles rigid and hard as he gave her his full strength and fucked her with everything that he had.

There were so many ways that he wanted to take her. Positions he'd read about that he wanted to try. Places on her voluptuous little body that he wanted to explore, invade and lay claim to.

Letting her nipple go with a soft, wet pop of sound, he surged up over her, the hard planes of his chest pressing against the soft swells of her breasts. "Sam," he groaned, lowering his forehead to hers. "Only you have...this power over me. I didn't know it would be like this. I didn't know."

"And that's a good thing?" she asked breathlessly.

"Oh yeah," he admitted in a low, rumbling drawl. "I admit that it scares the hell out of me because now I have something that I want to keep so badly, that I can't even imagine losing it but I wouldn't trade the feelings for anything."

"Yeah," she panted, her smile so sweet and vulnerable, "me too."

"You know we're going to be lucky if we can walk tomorrow," he growled, giving her a hard smile, his body moving even harder within her.

"I don't care," she moaned, face flushed brilliant and dark as her white teeth sank into the fullness of her lower lip. "I've always thought walking was overrated anyways," she added playfully, the look in her eyes daring him to give her everything.

His woman had asked him to show her, to show her just how much he wanted her, how much of an animal he could be.

And with the knowledge that he'd fallen helplessly in love with her, Four spent the rest of the night doing just that.

Chapter Eleven
Under the Right Circumstances

ନ୍ଦ

"Your feet are cold," Jerri murmured as Deuce opened his eyes.

She'd woken a few minutes earlier and had spent the time watching her lover as he'd slept. Even asleep, he looked powerful. He had certainly proved powerful last night in bed. He'd challenged her, earlier in the evening, to see what she could get out of him and she'd more than met the challenge, pulling one orgasm after another out of his strong, muscular body.

Of course, he'd done the same for her.

Deuce shifted beside her on the bed. Beneath the crisp sheets, his icy-cold foot slid across her shin as he moved his knee between her legs and planted an elbow beside her shoulder. Leaning over her, he smiled down at her out of sleepy blue eyes. "Well you know what they say," he drawled, "cold feet…warm cock."

Jerri giggled. "That's not what they say, you adorably handsome brute," she teased.

He nuzzled his lips into the warm place behind her ear. "No?"

"No. The saying is cold hands, warm heart."

"Mmph," he murmured. "I think I like my saying better but do you want to check out my hands?" Lifting his head to look down on her again, he brushed his knuckles across her lips. "What do you think?"

"They're warm," she told him, smiling sulkily.

"Well you know what they say," he drawled again, "warm hands, hot cock."

"That is *not* what they say!" she laughed out loud. "You've got it wrong again!"

The corner of his mouth kicked up into a heartwarming smile. "We've rewritten things a bit in the future," Deuce chuckled.

"Well, that's obvious! And it's pretty damn apparent that it was men who were doing all the rewriting!"

His smile drooped at little as his expression turned serious.

Jerri lifted a finger and traced out the border of the black skin surrounding his left eye. "What's wrong?" she asked.

With lightning-like reflexes he captured her hand, pulling it away from the sensitive flesh rimming his eye. Curling her fingers around his thumb, he pressed his lips to her knuckles. "It's ten o'clock in the morning on Monday, July twenty-fourth," he answered. "The Health Department has been open for two hours."

"Health department?" Jerri shook her head. Her thick hair rustled on the pillow beneath her.

Deuce released her hand, moving to sit on the edge of the bed. "We need to get to the County Health Department."

"Why?" Jerri watched him stand and reach for his jeans on the chair beside the bed. "Does this have anything to do with the poison gas?"

He jerked his chin in a nod. "Even if we stop the robbery tomorrow, the gas is still a threat." He shrugged. "After we change the future, we'll have no idea what happens next. For all we know, there'll be another robbery attempt — the next day, the next week, the next year. We have to get the Health Department involved."

"Why not just go to Janus and…"

"And what?" he asked, pulling his jeans up his legs. His cock was semi-rigid, long and as thick as a heavily-corded rope. He tucked it inside his pants then started working on the metal buttons on his fly. "You want us to go to Janus wearing masks and explain that we're from the future? Tell him we know his gas canisters are filled with poison? That he needs to remove them immediately?" Sweeping his shoes off the floor, he sat down on the bed. With one ankle resting on his knee, he slipped a shoe over his foot.

"Socks," she reminded him.

Deuce muttered a low curse under his breath, his brows pulled together in a look of mild irritation. "After last night, there's no reason for me not to tell you that I want to be able to slip my shoes on and off quickly," he grumbled.

She gave him a soft smile. "Socks won't slow you down too much and if we're going to be walking a lot today, those shoes will give you blisters."

He thought for a moment, then nodded and crossed the room in search of his socks. "If we were to go to Janus," he said, returning to the topic of discussion, "what do you suppose he would think?"

Jerri propped herself up on the mound of pillows, the soft sheet resting low across her chest. "He'd probably think you were trying to have the canisters removed so that you could steal the mercoldium masks," she admitted around a small yawn.

"That's right," he answered from across the room, hopping in place as he pulled a sock over his ankle and eyed her nipples beneath the fine cotton sheet. "We don't want to do anything that would draw attention to ourselves, anything that would result in our surveillance or anything that might land us in jail and jeopardize our mission."

Jerri nodded. "What about the Health Department? Won't a visit to the Health Department be drawing attention to yourselves?"

"It might," Deuce grunted, "except that you and Sam are going to make that visit for us."

"*We are?*"

Slipping his feet into his shoes, he nodded and pulled out the chair that was tucked beneath a mahogany desk built against the wall. "That's right," he said, tugging a small notepad in front of him and dropping into the chair. He picked up a pen, studied it doubtfully, turned it over in his hands and slanted a look at Jerri. "Where's the starter?" he asked.

"Starter?" Jerri asked, grinning as her amusement got the better of her. "It, uh, doesn't have a starter. You just press it against the paper and it writes. It makes marks," she supplied helpfully. "Blue marks," she added as she giggled.

Tentatively, Deuce pressed the pen's tip against the white notepad. After a few strokes, he flashed a grin at Jerri and continued.

Moments later Kar'four stepped through the door from Sam's room, adjusting his silver mask over his right eye. Jerri tugged the white sheets up to her neck, then grabbed at the duvet and pulled it up too, for good measure. "Don't you ever knock?" she groused.

"Knock?" he asked as he sauntered across the room. "What's that? It sounds sexy."

Jerri snorted. "Yeah," she grumbled good-naturedly. "Well if *you* did it, it probably *would* be sexy. It's when you bang on the door with your fist before you barge into somebody's bedroom. Don't they knock in the future?"

"Not if the door is unlocked," Four explained blandly. "Is there a reason behind this...knocking?"

"Yes," Jerri told him primly. "It's so you don't walk in on somebody while they're—" Jerri stopped, remembering that nobody wore clothes in the future. "Oh never mind," she laughed.

Deuce smiled at his brother. "Take a look at this," he told Kar'four. "It's a..." He looked to Jerri for help.

"It's a pen," she told him, hiding her grin behind the eyelet duvet.

Kar'four stepped across the room to check it out. "You're outlining the process that transformed the gas?" he asked.

Deuce nodded. "We'll have the girls take the notes into the Health Department while we wait outside."

A worried frown creased Four's brow. With one hand, he pushed back the dark hair that spilled across his forehead. "Do you think they'll believe it?"

"I'm just hoping they understand it! You can check my work," he commanded his brother. "If they have a staff epidemiologist, he should be able to follow my notes."

"Or she," Jerri interjected from the bed.

Both men stopped to stare at her.

"The epidemiologist could be a woman," Jerri reminded them.

The two brothers turned to stare at one another. "I think you just made your first chauvinistic blunder," Kar'four snorted.

Deuce leaned back to lock his accusatory gaze on Jerri. "Give us a chance, darling. We're hardly used to the idea that women *exist*, let alone the possibility that they occupy positions of authority!"

Jerri muffled her giggles beneath the duvet while the men returned to business.

"Are you hoping the Health Department will get the canisters changed before the robbery occurs?" Four queried.

Deuce grimaced. "Not really. But even if we stop the robbery, the canisters need to be removed as soon as possible."

"What's the plan for stopping the robbery?" Sam's voice intruded into the room.

Kar'four turned to smile at Sam, who was wrapped in a long black satin robe and leaning against the doorjamb. "We know the robbery takes place tomorrow morning between ten and eleven o'clock. We know where the masks are. We'll position ourselves so that we can watch the masks and intercept the thieves before they reach them."

Sam's eyes widened a notch. "That's it? That's the plan?"

Kar'four looked askance. "What's wrong with it?"

"I just thought you'd have more information about the...perpetrators...the method. I thought you'd know who the thieves were, what they looked like and exactly how to stop them."

Four shook his head. "A lot of the eyewitnesses died." He cleared his throat. "Approximately half of them. And it was almost fifty years after the robbery before the masks were even retrieved."

"And they never got any sort of confession or statements out of the thieves," Sam finished for him.

Kar'four shook his head. "No. No statements. No details. The masks might never even have been discovered, except for a random gravimetric flyover of a large graveyard in Ohio."

"The masks were buried in a graveyard? *Priceless mercoldium masks*? Let me guess. The thieves didn't live long enough to enjoy their ill-gotten gains? Serves the bastards right. So what do we know about these guys?"

Kar'four's smile was sad. "Well," he said quietly. "About all that could be told from the fifty-year-old skeletons was that the thieves were...women. Needless to say, they died within ten days of the robbery. We think they were blonde."

* * * * *

Deuce was introspectively quiet as he rode down in the elevator with Jerri at his side. Sam had been dragging her heels and Jerri's lover was too anxious to hang about the room, waiting for the other couple. He needed more room to pace, so he and Jerri had left them to follow when they were ready.

"What time is it?" he asked tersely as the elevator doors opened.

Jerri glanced at her wristwatch and stepped out of the elevator into the huge lobby on the casino's main level. "Eleven o'clock," she told him, her voice apologetic as she glanced around at the beautiful floors of white marble laced with thin stringers of sparkling gold. In the center of the expansive lobby sat an indoor lake. Overhead, the domed ceiling glittered rich gold while a distant circle placed at the dome's center gleamed warm silver.

"I hope they hurry up," he muttered under his breath. "We need to get to the Health Department before everyone breaks for lunch."

Jerri nodded as she squeezed his hand. "There they are!" she exclaimed, pointing across the lobby.

Deuce frowned. "Where?"

Leaving him in front of the elevators, Jerri started out across the polished marble floor. "Over there. I just saw Four. He stepped behind that column. Come on."

Deuce followed uncertainly, turning back to eye the long bank of elevator doors. "I don't see how they could have…"

An elevator door parted and Sam stepped through with Kar'four following her. "Jerri," Deuce shouted, "here they are!"

Jerri frowned as she turned, a quizzical expression rumpling her brow. She glanced once more across the lobby then returned to join Deuce and the others moving toward the casino's exit. Deuce slowed his steps to intercept hers, wrapping an arm around her waist and tugging her into his side. She opened her mouth to say something about the man she'd seen who looked so much like the two handsome clones but got distracted when her gaze snagged on Kar'four's apparel. "Nice shirt," she told Four, giving him a broad wink.

Sam gave her a smile. "He looks hot, doesn't he?"

Sam's lover was still wearing his vintage jeans and high pirate boots. Having lost his black duster in the fall the night before, he'd borrowed one of Sam's larger shirts, which apparently hadn't been quite large enough. He'd torn the sleeves out to make room for his broad shoulders. The buttons wouldn't quite meet across his chest but a few of the lower ones were fastened. Open almost to his navel and torn at the shoulders, the shirt made Four the quintessential pirate.

"All he needs is a parrot," Jerri agreed, sending her friend a grin.

Sam was still smiling her concurrence as the huge sliding glass doors slipped open to let them through and they stepped out into the dry heat of the Nevada desert.

The sidewalks were relatively empty, the midday heat driving most of the tourists into the cool casinos lining the wide boulevard. Almost alone on the street, the foursome was a tempting target for the city's ever-present population of streetwalkers. The two couples hadn't traveled three blocks before they were accosted by a very persistent male prostitute.

"Eighty bucks a ride," the young man offered, dogging the two couples as they made their way down the street. "Two hundred fer the lot of ya." He was dressed in an outrageously scanty western costume, his white leather chaps trailing long fringes that dragged on the concrete sidewalk. His chest was bare. His cowboy hat was red. The G-string that pocketed his sex matched his hat. It glittered with red sequins.

Sam rolled her eyes while Jerri blushed like a rose.

"We're not your type," Deuce advised the young streetwalker.

The young man hurried to get himself in front of them, back pedaling as he targeted Sam and Jerri as the recipients of his charms. "I ain't got a type," he insisted. "One hundred then, just fer the gals. The fellas can watch, no charge."

"*Not* interested," Jerri insisted in a tight voice.

"Is he bothering you?" Deuce questioned mildly.

"Yes!" Jerri returned from the side of her mouth. *"What do you think? A male prostitute is hitting on me!"*

Deuce grinned. "Sorry. I'm more used to them hitting on me…or Four."

"Why don't you do something?" she ground out of the corner of her mouth.

"Aw," he drawled. "I wouldn't want to hurt the little darling. Leave him be, Jerri. The poor lad's just trying to make a living."

"That's right," the prostitute parroted, "just tryin' a make a living."

"Hang on." Sam stopped in the middle of the sidewalk, fishing inside her purse. She pulled out a rumpled fifty-dollar bill and waved it like a flag under the young man's nose. "Here's a fifty. See that woman across the street? The one with the blonde hair and the red vinyl duster?"

Everyone stopped to stare across the road and find the woman in question, who stood eyeing the stylish merchandise displayed in an upscale boutique window.

"Why don't you give her a full ten minutes of your undivided attention?" Sam suggested. "And if you can get her into bed you'll earn another fifty."

"Sam!" Jerri croaked, eyes round with surprise.

The prostitute licked his lips. His cautious gaze flicked across the wide street then back to the fifty. "How will yer know if I fucked her or not?"

Sam's eyes gleamed. "You'll bring me that red vinyl duster she's wearing."

"Right," he said slowly. "Right." He snatched the fifty out of Sam's fingers. "Where do I bring it?"

"Room 1623 at the Palace."

The young man tucked the bill into the front of his G-string, looked both ways before he crossed the road, then jogged across the gray asphalt.

"Can we *afford* another fifty?" Jerri asked her friend as they resumed their trek to the Health Department.

"I don't care if we can or not," Sam muttered through clenched teeth. "I want that damn duster back."

* * * * *

Ten minutes later, they arrived at the Health Department. While the men waited out front, Sam and Jerri requested a counter-top meeting with the epidemiologist. Although they were relieved to learn that he was in and available to meet with them, they were both nervous. The harried civil servant was skeptical at first—more than skeptical—but he came around a bit after he saw Deuce's notes.

"Well," he finally allowed, "if this is the biological agent originally used in those canisters, I can see how this sort of transformation might take place, under the right circumstances of heat and pressure."

"The canisters must be removed," Jerri pressed him.

The man frowned as he pulled a hand back through his bushy, graying hair.

"And they must never be opened after their removal," Sam added.

He nodded. "The canisters can be destroyed easily enough, along with the gas inside them." Again he nodded. He took off his glasses, folded them and slid them into his shirt pocket, alongside a bleeding felt tip pen that he'd apparently forgotten to cap. "We'll have to make inquiries, make certain that this is, in fact, the gas that was used in the canisters. If we can establish that fact, then I think we can issue an order and require their removal from Janus Palace. I'll 'red code' the inquiry, giving it emergency priority so that it will be dealt with as seriously as though it were an outbreak of the Ebola virus." He peered at the women, his expression interested. "But tell me, how did you stumble across this...this...revelation?"

Sam stared at him. Obviously, she hadn't anticipated this question.

"Master's thesis," Jerri blurted out.

The epidemiologist focused his attention on Jerri.

"Uh…we were studying the efficacy of sleeping gas agents. We…got to fiddling with the…erm…organic chemistry involved, applying different conditions and…and…that's what we came up with. Right, Sam?"

Sam looked stunned for just an instant then nodded vigorously. Humor, along with proud admiration, shone in her green eyes.

A few minutes later the two women were hurrying through the Health Department doors again.

"Efficacy?" Sam teased her friend, grimacing as she laughed. "Is that even a word?"

"I think so," Jerri returned with a low chuckle, her expression wry.

Sam punched her friend lightly on the shoulder. "You done good, Jerri."

"Thank *god* for 'word of the day' calendars."

"Actually," Sam drawled, "you should probably thank your 'Ocean Mother'."

"'By the skies', you're right!" Jerri laughed. "Either that or my Ocean Lover."

Deuce swept up behind her and wrapped her up in a hug. "Talking about me?" he murmured against her ear. He turned Jerri around to face him. "How'd they take the news?" he asked more seriously.

Jerri gave him a bright smile. "I think they're going to help."

Chapter Twelve
A Regular Little Klepto

∞

The desert sun burned mercilessly within the deep blue of the sky, the waves of stifling heat rising from the cracked concrete beneath their feet and slithering up their legs, making their limbs feel heavy as they stood outside the front doors of the Health Department.

Shielding her eyes from the bright glare, Jerri looked up at Deuce. The sun glinted off his silvery metal mask in a brilliant, blinding kaleidoscope of colors, putting the rest of his features into shadow. "So what now?" she asked, trying to determine his expression.

Before he could answer, Sam said, "I say we head back to the hotel and get out of this damn heat before I'm fried to a crisp."

"Hmm…" Four murmured thoughtfully as he pulled her into his side, one muscled arm latched firmly and possessively around her waist. "I guess we could always go back to the rooms and lose ourselves in some more mind-blowing sex while we plan the next move."

The corner of Sam's mouth twitched as she met Four's playful, smoldering stare. "Oh yeah? And what's the next move?"

"Do a walk-through of tomorrow's crime scene. Maybe get some food. Fuck your brains out and make you scream my name like a banshee." The last was delivered with a purely piratical smile that would have made any woman's toes curl.

Obviously no exception, Sam's knees went weak. "That's some plan," she said breathlessly.

Flashing his own boyish grin, Deuce gave a low laugh. "Four has always been our best strategist."

"And what are you best at?" Jerri teased, still shielding her eyes as she stared up at him. The warm, spicy scent of his body rose on the desert air, making her mouth water for a taste of him. She didn't know how it had happened but in such a short time he'd become something so necessary to her, just like air and water.

"What am I best at?" Feigning a hurt look of surprise, he arched one dark brow. "I would have thought that was obvious, woman."

Four snickered while the two women laughed.

"Doesn't matter how evolved they are," Sam delivered with a sarcastic snort, "men still haven't managed to outgrow the need to have their egos stroked."

"I've got something you can stroke," Four growled, lifting her off her feet to spin her in a dizzying circle.

When they came to a stop, they both swayed where they stood.

Putting a hand to her burning forehead, Sam fanned her flushed face with the other. "Back to the hotel, *now* or they'll be carting our sad bodies off to the hospital when we all pass out from heat stroke."

Smiling, the group set off down the sidewalk. By the time they reached the Janus, they were hot, hungry and edgy with nervous energy. Once in Sam's room, they dug out the room service menus and ordered what seemed like one of everything, along with four ice-cold beers. Compared to the sweltering, tourist-packed streets of the city, the luxurious hotel room was cool and calm, a soothing balm to the group's restless energy. Housekeeping had tidied up while they were gone and now the bed once again resembled the picture-perfect symmetry of an interior design magazine.

Deuce sat at the desk as Jerri kneaded the knotted tension in his broad shoulders, while Sam walked to the far window, its curtains pulled aside to reveal the endless expanse of the desert that stretched beyond the mammoth heights of the city. Janus Palace rose higher than any of its surrounding buildings, affording her an uninterrupted view of the stark, yet strangely beautiful landscape. Coming up behind her, Four wrapped his arms around her middle and pulled her back against the solid heat of his chest. His head lowered and he nuzzled the side of her throat, just beneath her ear.

"Do you know how much I want you?" he whispered huskily.

Wiggling her bottom against the generous swell of his groin, she smiled at his reflection in the glass. "How many guesses am I allowed?"

"I'd allow you anything, Sam." His arms tightened, holding her closer. "Anything but allowing another to touch you—to touch what's mine."

Letting her head fall back against his shoulder, she looked up at him. "I don't want any other man to touch me, Four."

Hardening his jaw, he looked away to stare out over the fabulous desert city that grew like a jewel in the middle of nowhere. "You will, if I can't stay," he gritted through his teeth, the words guttural and deep. "If I'm gone, you'll forget me."

In a soft, wistful voice, she said, "Let's not talk about what-ifs, okay?"

His hands moved, one rough palm cupping the heavy swell of one breast, while the other cupped her mound. "I can't," he admitted gruffly. "You were right when you said I wanted to mark you, Sam. I do. I want to put my mark, my scent, my claim all over you. I want every man who gets near you to know that you're taken. That I'm the only man you'll spread those beautiful thighs for. The only man allowed to open the tender lips of your cunt and lick up your cream. I want to carry that sugar sweet taste with me everywhere, Sam.

I want it always. I want…I just want…I want to keep you. Own you."

She trembled and he pressed forward, pushing until her shirt-covered breasts flattened against the cool window, making her gasp. "If we were alone, I'd take you right here, Sam," he whispered in her ear. "I'd strip those irritating clothes away and press your lush, beautiful body against this window and I'd fuck you. I'd fuck you *hard*, without caring who was watching out of those thousands of windows out there. I'd fuck you so hard that you couldn't breathe, could do nothing but sob my name over and over, begging for more, and every man out there would see just how completely you belong to me."

"I've read scenes like that," she panted, the words hoarse, "in books."

Kar'four ran his teeth down the tender tendon that connected her neck and shoulder. "Me too."

Their lust-darkened eyes met in the reflection on the window, searing blue and hazy green. His strong fingers found the top button of her jeans, popping it free. Her legs trembled, chest heaving. Behind her, his muscles tightened, pressing her forward the barest inch, daring her to call a halt to his actions.

In the clear glass, with the skin across his high cheekbones pulled tight, firm lips parted the barest fraction, eyes burning with heat, his expression could only be described as hard with determination and lust. "I want to ruin you for other men," he snarled, the words almost violent in their intensity. "Forever."

"You already have," she moaned.

He grunted in response, the second button breaking free then the third, when a loud, cracking knock echoed through the room.

"Fuck," he cursed under his breath.

"Um, that should be the food," Jerri murmured. "I'll get the door."

Sam and Four moved apart, expecting to see one of the immaculately dressed hotel staff wheeling in a cart. Only, when the door pulled open, no waiter stood in the hallway. Instead, they found the sass-talking streetwalker from earlier that morning, wearing nothing but a smile...and a red vinyl duster.

Sam hurried to fasten the top three buttons on her jeans while she stared at the young blond standing in the open doorway. His arms were spread wide, exposing his freckled chest...and everything else from there on down to his toes.

"Got yer coat," he announced, grinning widely.

Jerri's brown eyes were shocked wide as she stared at him. "Did you have to trade the rest of your clothing to get it?" She looked behind him as though expecting his chaps, hat and sequined G-string to follow him into the room.

"Nah," he explained, looking at Jerri as though she were nuts. "I dint trade 'em. I lost 'em!"

Again, Jerri looked behind him. "Lost them! What did they do? Fall off your ass?"

He shook his head. "The blonde lady. She stole 'em. She's a regular little klepto. I reckon she'd have stolen my balls if they weren't screwed on tight." He reached for his groin as if to demonstrate the fact that his equipment was, in fact, still intact but Deuce held a hand out like a stop sign.

"That *won't* be necessary," Deuce admonished the streetwalker with a barely contained smile.

"So," Kar'four asked, his eyes narrowing in disbelief. "While you were stealing her coat, she was making off with your cowboy suit?"

The prostitute's green eyes opened wide as he stared at Four. "'Course not! She made off with my clothes as well as the coat. I had to chase her two blocks to get the coat off'n her.

134

I'm lucky I didn't get nabbed fer indecent exposure." He grinned at the idea. "Tell ya what though. It was a good thing that coat was red. It's hard to hide in a bright red coat," he philosophized with a sage nod of his head.

The two men grinned back at him, nodding their concurrence. When Deuce held his hand out for the coat, the streetwalker shucked it off his shoulders as quickly as peeling bananas.

The two women gasped and averted their faces. Sam hurried for her purse, dug out a fifty and prodded the air behind her a few times before Four helped her out, plucking it from her blindly questing fingers.

"Thanks for the coat," Kar'four told the young man, delivering the fifty into his outstretched palm while Deuce opened the door for his exit.

Sam turned suddenly, her hands on her hips. "Wait a minute! He can't just go walking out there...naked!" she screeched.

Four sent both women a questioning look. "Why not?"

"Because," Jerri sputtered, "this is a hotel. A nice hotel!"

"*Your time* and its hang ups about clothing," Deuce laughed. "The body is a beautiful thing —"

"Like yers too, sugar," the prostitute snickered, winking at him.

Deuce crossed his arms and glared at the grinning streetwalker. "Will you just shut up for one second? I wasn't hitting on you, damn it!"

The blond waved a hand at him, gracelessly exaggerating the effeminate gesture. "Hey now, don't go getting testy, big boy."

"Sam," Four chuckled. "Get him some damn clothes and then get him outta here."

"Right," Sam agreed, already on the move. Stepping into the adjoining room, she swiftly returned with a pair of vintage blue jeans for the naked blond. He stepped into them while Deuce checked the pockets of the red vinyl duster.

"Already checked the pockets," the streetwalker informed him. "Ain't no money in them. Just some papers."

"Right," Deuce told him, pulling the papers from the pocket of the duster and throwing them on the bed's eyelet duvet. "Thanks for your help."

"You need anything else, just ask anyone on the street for the cowboy."

"Right," Four answered, herding him toward the door. "But I don't expect we'll be needing you."

The persistent young man was still talking as Kar'four backed him through the door. "Give my name to the rest of yer brothers!"

"We'll do that," Four growled, closing the door on his face. With a sigh, he gave his brother a wry smile as he leaned back against the door. "He was...persistent," Kar'four said.

Deuce tilted his head, his expression quizzical. "I wonder how he knew about our brothers."

Four shrugged one shoulder dismissively. "He was probably just *hoping* we had more brothers."

"Yeah," Deuce agreed with a considering nod.

There was another knock on the door and Kar'four rolled his eyes in exasperation as he jerked the door open again, barking, "What now?"

He flushed, mumbled an awkward apology under his breath and then stepped quickly aside for the wide-eyed, white-clad waiter who rolled in a long cart loaded with covered plates.

After the waiter left, Sam and Jerri pulled the ivory duvet from the bed and spread it in the middle of the sapphire rug. Preparing for a hotel room picnic, the women uncovered the various dishes as the delicate scent of crisp spring rolls blended pleasantly with the spicy aroma of chicken quesadillas. Deuce pulled four chilled bottles of beer from the ice bucket and passed them around. When everyone had a plate of food and an icy cold beer, the women sat cross-legged on the floor while the two men lounged at their sides.

Four's eyes dimmed with lust as his gaze got caught between Sam's legs. *Damn twenty-first century clothing*, he thought with a quiet snarl. It was always getting in the way. He wondered if Sam's sweet, succulent lips were parted inside her jeans, baring her precious pearl or if they kissed each other instead in a coy pout, hiding her secret folds and her tender opening. Trapped inside the constricting blue denim that wrapped his hips, Kar'four felt as though his cock was suffocating. He popped the top three buttons on his fly, just to give the poor thing room to breathe. "Couldn't we just do this naked?" he suggested in a lusty murmur. "It would be a lot more comfortable."

"We can get comfortable *after* we eat," Sam chided as she slanted him a look from beneath her lashes, her green eyes hazy with interest, even though she was obviously fighting the idea. "If we get comfortable now, the food will be cold before we finish getting comfortable."

Deuce and Jerri grinned at the exchange, while Four nodded absently, making plans to have Sam sitting cross-legged like that as soon as he had her stripped bare. In the meantime, he was starving. He bit into a shrimp purse, his eyes still focused between Sam's legs.

"You're drooling," Sam advised him. She reached for a wad of folded papers. When she realized they weren't napkins, she threw them aside. Locating some cloth napkins on the rolling cart, she retrieved them, using the edge of one napkin to dab at the corner of Kar'four's mouth.

"You could have just licked it off," he pointed out.

She sat back on her ankles with a smirking smile. "Now, why didn't I think of that?"

"It's not too late," he murmured, leaning in for a short kiss. "My mouth isn't the only thing that's drooling."

"I'll take care of that right after lunch," she promised, sealing the bargain with a sultry wink.

"What's this?" Four asked, his interest suddenly drawn to the wadded papers at the edge of the duvet.

"What's what?" Sam asked.

He picked up the folded papers, turned them over and opened them. "Why do you have a floor plan of the palace?"

"A floor plan of the..." Sam stared at the papers. "That's not my floor plan. It's the blonde's floor plan. It was in the pocket of that red duster."

Chapter Thirteen
The Interference Factor

§೧

Silence reigned in room 1623 as the two couples slowly gravitated toward the same conclusion.

"It's the blonde's floor plan," Sam repeated, her green eyes wide with realization.

"It was in the pocket of that duster she stole," Jerri murmured.

"A floor plan of Janus Palace," Four stated with distant wonder.

"The thieves who stole the mercoldium masks were thought to be blonde," Deuce contributed, before continuing slowly, "I think…"

"We just found our robbers," all four of them said together.

For several seconds they stared at each other, the silence heavy and thick with the churning weight of their thoughts.

"Or at least one of them," Sam pointed out sensibly, after a moment.

Jerri's gaze moved from Sam to Deuce. His lips were pressed together with tightly held tension as he flicked his troubled gaze at his brother.

"What?" Sam asked, her frown deepening as she considered first one man then the other.

"What is it?" Jerri joined in, not liking the concern that shadowed her lover's face.

It was Kar'four who finally answered. He tilted his head in a defensive shrug. "The interference factor," he stated with obvious reluctance.

"Interference factor?"

Kar'four rolled up to sit on his heels, buttoning his fly absently while explaining, "We came here planning to stop a robbery which was to take place on the morning of the twenty-fifth — tomorrow morning."

"And..." Sam invited him to continue.

"If that blonde kleptomaniac is one of the robbers," Deuce cut in with a dissatisfied growl, "there's a good chance we've interfered with the circumstances leading up to the event."

"So what?" Sam shot at Deuce impatiently. "Now we know what one of the thieves looks like. All we have to do is keep our eye on her, find out who her accomplice is and watch them both. The minute they make their move toward the masks, we nail them."

"Yes," Deuce agreed, his tone critical. "That would be nice."

At Sam's side, Kar'four bristled. "Don't jump on Sam," he snapped at his brother. "She hasn't had as long to think about this as we have. She hasn't had the benefit of a whole cartload of scientists sitting around for the last two hundred years, coming up with different scenarios!"

Deuce's tense glare softened a hairsbreadth as he accepted this information with a nod. When he levered himself into a sitting position, Jerri shifted to her knees behind him. She smoothed her palms over his shoulders, attempting to soothe the tension out of her lover's long, hard frame.

"Deuce," she encouraged him gently.

He tilted his head, smiling back at her, his volatile blue gaze warming with affection as he sighed. "The scientists warned us that we should 'sit tight' when we got here. Check out the location of the robbery then stay hidden and out of view until the time of the theft. They were concerned that any *activity* on our part might interfere with the…time line leading up to the crime."

Sam shifted impatiently and Jerri shot her friend a quick glance of warning while she kneaded Deuce's shoulders. "And…" she coaxed him.

"Don't you see?" he explained. "Anything we might do could interfere with the robbery's outcome."

"Why would that necessarily be a bad thing?" she asked him quietly.

"If our actions interfere, then the robbery might not take place tomorrow. The thieves might disappear."

"And that would be a bad thing?" Sam scoffed.

"Yes," Four explained gently. "Just because the theft doesn't happen tomorrow doesn't mean it won't happen eventually. Which means, if we can't get the Health Department to remove the canisters, we might have to spend the rest of our lives here at the Palace, watching day and night, waiting for the robbery to take place."

"And that's the best-case scenario," Deuce stated, moving suddenly to his feet.

Sam stared up at him from her place on the floor. "What's the worst-case scenario?" she demanded bluntly.

The lines around Deuce's mouth tightened. He lifted one dark eyebrow, as much as to say, 'figure it out, yourself'.

Sam gave him a blank look as she shook her head.

The answer came from Jerri. Her eyes were fixed on the floor plan lying at the edge of the duvet. "The thieves get nervous," she stated slowly, "and decide to steal the masks today."

This unsettling revelation was followed by a sharp, impatient pounding on the hotel room door. Everyone in the room froze for a few instants, staring at the door as though their worst fears might somehow stand just beyond it. From the corridor outside there issued a muffled voice, deep and urgent. "Four. Two. Open up."

Jerri watched as Sam's eyes narrowed in wonder. At the same time, shock stunned the features of their handsome lovers. Despite this fact, Jerri found the deep voice so reassuringly familiar, that she moved toward the door without either fear or hesitation. What she found on the other side was pretty much what she'd expected, despite the improbability of the whole situation. For when Jerri opened the door, two men stepped through the opening, each of them a near-perfect replica of her lover, Deuce. And the second one, damn him, had the audacity to sweep her into his arms and nail her with a long, enthusiastic kiss.

For several seconds, Four and Deuce stared at their brothers while Jerri stood just inside the door, breathlessly caught up in the arms of a man who looked astonishingly like her lover. In fact, if it weren't for the absence of either a mask *or* dark leathery skin on the left side of his face, Jerri might not have known the man from his brother, Deuce. Of course, the knitted cap he had pulled down over his ears helped.

"Get your hands off my woman, Tré," Deuce suddenly grumbled, finally breaking the silence.

While Deuce glared at the grinning offender, whose strong arms pulled a stunned Jerri tighter against his tall body, Kar'four's dark gaze traveled over the newcomers. "Where'd you get the clothes?" he asked, his awe evident in his puzzled tone, as though it were the most compelling question in the universe.

The other brother chuckled, tugging at the brim of his straw cowboy hat. "You're not the only ones walking around on millions, Four. The clothes were easy enough to buy, once we found a..."

"Pawn shop," Tré supplied.

"Once we found a pawn shop and got our hands on the right currency." A slow, crooked smile spread across his mouth. "It was hardly fair to the ladies, flashing them our manly attributes when there's not enough time to give them all a taste of the goods. And I can't believe we travel two hundred years back in time to be with you and all you think to ask us is where our clothes came from!"

"Okay," Four growled. "What are you doing here, Ace? No, wait!" he muttered, his expression suddenly concerned. "Where's Kar'five? And Six?"

"They're watching the masks," Tré answered swiftly. "We think something's about to happen."

Kar'four's face dropped. "Then we've failed?" he asked in a low voice of defeat. "You were sent out after us because nothing changed after we left? And you knew we'd failed?"

"Don't be ridiculous," Ace answered, bending down to pick up a shrimp purse from the picnic spread then tossing it up in the air to catch it in his open mouth. He laughed at his own trick as he chewed, eyeing Four and Deuce. "We went out the night before you did, to watch you, to watch the masks, to make sure you *didn't* fail."

After a quick glance at Deuce, Four nodded. "Yeah, that makes sense. I don't know why we didn't expect it."

Picking up another crisp golden puff, Ace shrugged his broad shoulders. "You had other things on your mind." He shot a grinning glance at the women. "And once you got here, trust me, we more than understood your lapse in attention."

"We didn't lapse in anything," Deuce muttered, stepping forward to pull Jerri out of Tré's tight embrace, then securing her at his side with one arm wrapped possessively around her waist. "We've identified one of the thieves!"

"*And* we've been to the Health Department," Four added, his expression as defensive as Deuce's.

"Oh! And I saw you down in the lobby!" Jerri exclaimed, her expression smug as she snuggled closer to Deuce, wrapping her arms around his lean waist in a show of support. Her gaze moved from Ace to Tré. Slowly, her head tilted to the side as she studied him, her soft mouth puckering into a thoughtful moue. "Or maybe it was him. But he…wasn't wearing a hat," she said uncertainly. Her shoulders lifted and she laughed as she looked up at her lover, capturing his warm gaze. "To be honest, I don't know how you tell them apart," she confessed, looking a little embarrassed.

Ace gave his companion a stern look while Tré hurried to defend himself. "It wasn't me. It was probably Sixpack."

"Once you learn their different attitudes and expressions," Deuce responded, grinning as he leaned down to press a kiss to her temple, "telling them apart just comes naturally."

"And Kar'one is always easy to identify," Four explained, eyeing Ace, his voice tight with irritation. "Because he's the perfectionist of the bunch, always criticizing how other people do their jobs."

Rising from his crouch, Ace wiped his hands on the heavy corduroy of his slacks while the corners of his wide mouth turned down. "Damn it, I wasn't criticizing you."

"Sounded like criticism to me," Tré chuckled. "I think you should kick his —"

"I'd like to see him try," Ace growled.

"Ace is just jealous," Tré continued to prod, grinning as he stared at his brothers. "He about turned green with envy when he saw these two beauties attack your sorry asses and spirit you off to their rooms."

Sam crossed her arms over her chest. "We were *helping* them," she muttered, glaring at the smirking example of masculine perfection. "Not attacking them!"

Tré's blue eyes turned bright with interest. "I could have used some 'help' like that," he teasingly drawled.

"Don't even think about it," Deuce growled at the same time Jerri blurted, "We had to help them. They were naked! Their parts were hanging out for everyone to see!"

She blushed crimson when four sets of electric blue eyes turned her way. "Well, they were," she mumbled, crossing her arms to imitate Sam's body language.

"And we've wandered way off topic," Kar'four drawled, hugging Sam to his front so that he could rest his chin upon her honey-brown hair, his strong arms wrapped just beneath her breasts. "Why did Five take watch duty with Sixpack? Everyone knows they fight like cats and dogs."

A low, rasping snicker echoed through the room, before Tré said, "They're being punished."

Four raised one dark brow, his expression questioning.

Tré crossed his arms over his broad chest as he leaned back against the wall. "You spent your last few days back at home with the scientists, so you weren't there for the fireworks. But there was a bit of an episode when Five's Synnie malfunctioned."

Both Four and Deuce groaned, while the women looked curious. "Again?" Deuce asked, shaking his head. "What'd he do to it this time?"

Ace shot him a wry look from his place across the room. "Tried to install another voice box."

"Those robot sex toy thingies can talk?" Sam questioned, while her eyes went wide with surprise.

Four shook his head. "Not really. Only prerecorded responses. Kinda creepy, if you ask me." He shuddered dramatically, as if in memory and Sam hid her smile behind her hand. "The voice boxes are an optional feature that you have to install yourself. And they almost always end in disaster."

"What did Five program it to say this time?" Deuce asked, the corner of his mouth already twitching with humor.

"*Oh* Five, you're *so* much bigger than your brothers," Tré drawled in a high, sing-song voice that made the women cringe, while the men busted up with laughter, the warm male sound echoing off the walls. "Five, Five, you're such a better lover than Ace and Tré and Deuce and—"

"Oh god," Four groaned, nearly choking. "I think we get the point."

"And I think the moral of this story is that you should *never* let a man put words in a woman's mouth," Jerri giggled.

Tré's grin flashed, a little lopsided and wickedly suggestive, as he stared at her soft smile. "And just what *should* we put in a woman's mouth, gorgeous?"

Deuce stopped laughing long enough to glare at his brother. "For the last time, stop flirting with my woman, you ass!"

"You get tired of this lug, you know where to find me," Tré drawled while sending her a wink, ignoring his brother's snarling growls.

"Stop baiting him," Kar'four snorted, sharing a grin with Tré, "and finish telling us what happened."

"The voice box caused another mal*function*." Ace winced on the last word, making Four and Deuce raise their brows.

"It caused an involuntary spasm that made the Synnie's feminine bits clamp down on him," he grimaced as he explained, "while Five was, uh, in mid-stroke."

"Ouch!" Sam gasped, while the brothers all shuddered, groaning in sympathy.

Tré took up the telling of the story again. "Sixpack heard him shouting, ran in to help and offered his assistance by yanking the Synnie off of him. Said Five's dick stretched out *this* far," he explained, laughing huskily and holding his hands spread wide in demonstration, "before it finally snapped free. And the whole time that damn thing was moaning, 'Five, Five, you make me feel so alive.' Sixpack said it was the funniest damn thing he'd ever seen."

"I bet Five didn't think so," Kar'four wheezed, wiping tears of laughter from the corners of his eyes.

"Yeah, well, when Five could finally walk without crying, he let Sixpack know firsthand with his fists just how much he appreciated his so-called help and they ended up destroying one of the labs in the process. Took both of us and the entire Bal family to pull them off each other."

"So the watch dog duty is part of their penance," Deuce said, smiling as he looked toward Ace. "I doubt Five will ever forgive you, brother."

The corner of Ace's mouth curled. "Five should just be happy that he's still all in one piece and fully functioning."

"There's something that I don't understand," Jerri murmured, drawing everyone's attention as she stared up at Deuce.

"What's that, baby?" he asked.

"Well, if all your brothers are here, why can't *they* stop the robbery? Why does it have to be you and Kar'four?"

Before Deuce could answer, Four said, "Because none of our brothers can fly."

"Or dive to thirty feet," Deuce added.

Jerri started to say something more, then paused, tilting her head as her eyes narrowed in confusion. "Fly? Dive to thirty feet? Wait a minute," she said slowly, looking from one brother to the other. "Exactly where *are* the mercoldium masks?"

Chapter Fourteen
Hidden in Plain View

છ્ડ

"The masks!" Tré shouted as though he'd just remembered the reason for the brothers' trip to the year 2050, along with their present visit to Sam and Jerri's rooms. "That's why we're here!" he exclaimed. "We think something's about to happen to the mercoldium masks."

Deuce's brow knitted with concern as he issued one short, gritty command. "Explain."

"We will," Ace told him. "But I think we'd better do it in the..."

"Elevator," Tré filled in.

"Five and Six might be able to delay the robbery from going down," Ace said swiftly. "But they won't be able to stop it."

"Delay the robbery?" Deuce growled. "You think it's going down *now*?"

Ace glared at his brother. "Don't yell at us," he barked. "You're the ones who interfered with the events leading up to the theft! It's not our fault the robbery is going down a day early!"

Deuce snarled out a groan of frustration. "If you think it's about to take place *now*, then why are we still standing here? Let's go!"

Hurrying through the hotel room doors and down the wide corridor, the party of six waited for an elevator to arrive, none of them more impatiently than Deuce. "By the seas," he muttered under his breath when a set of doors finally slid open.

Thankfully the car was empty.

As the four broad-shouldered men quickly filled the small space, Sam gave the crowded interior a doubtful look. "Jerri and I will just follow in the next one," she suggested.

Two sets of arms reached for the women as the elevator doors began to close, drawing them roughly against their lovers' hard frames. Four's hands slipped around to flatten Sam's bottom beneath his splayed fingers before her backside could create an obstruction and delay the closing of the elevator doors. Pinned between the mirrored doors and Kar'four's broad chest, Sam squirmed a bit before conceding in a muffled growl, "Or not."

Deuce flicked his gaze toward Ace. "Okay. Fill us in," he demanded.

"We got an alert from Five about fifteen minutes ago. He was down in the lobby with Sixpack, guarding the masks. A woman rode the escalator up from the convention level below. Five probably wouldn't have noticed her except for the fact that she looked remarkably like his Synnie back home." Ace paused to share a significant look with his brothers. "You know Five," he drawled. "The boy's always had a soft spot for that machine."

"Even after it almost took his cock off?"

Ace shrugged. "It was easier for him to blame Sixpack than to fault his precious Synnie. Anyhow," Ace continued, "the woman met what appeared to be an older sister over at the elevators. Five said the older one seemed to be a bit of a bitch. Almost immediately, she started pushing the younger one around."

Kar'four growled a private message to Sam. "Sound familiar?"

"All too much so," Sam muttered under her breath. "I should have kicked that kleptomaniac's skinny little troublemaking ass when I had the chance."

Ace gave the pair a quick glance before continuing. "Her sister, if that's what she was, rolled out a large round shipment container and together they started setting up a small display booth right next to the artificial lake."

"Right there in the lobby?" Four clarified.

"Right," Tré affirmed. "A couple of security guards came over and tried to redirect the women downstairs to the convention level but the women insisted they were VIP's and argued that they needed the high ceiling in the lobby to demonstrate their product."

"High ceiling?" Four echoed, his voice tight with concern. "What the hell were they selling?"

"*Elevator shoes,*" Tré said, enunciating the words significantly, as though condemning the women on the basis of those two words alone.

A few seconds of silence followed as the elevator car glided down another ten or twenty feet.

"Elevator shoes!" Sam echoed, her voice muffled by Four's hard chest. "What on earth is so suspicious about elevator shoes?" She hesitated while the car continued to drop silently downward. "Oh for heavens sake, you guys don't think that elevator shoes actually act like…elevators! Elevator shoes are just shoes with thick soles that make short people taller!"

"Then why did they need the higher ceilings?" Jerri queried with quiet concern. "Why did they insist on setting up their booth in the lobby?"

The tight space inside the packed car grew heavy with silence as Sam mentally chewed on this idea. In fact, she wanted to grind the whole concept between her back molars, mash it into a pulp and spit it out. She wanted to reject the idea completely. She wasn't ready for the robbery to happen today—not right now! It was supposed to happen tomorrow!

She'd thought she would have another night—another glorious night with Kar'four—to prepare herself for both the theft and the events that might follow. There were two possible outcomes and both of them scared her to death. If Deuce and Four failed to stop the robbery, Sam and Jerri were looking at their own deaths within ten days. If, on the other hand, the brothers were successful in preventing the theft, they had to concern themselves with the idea that their handsome lovers, along with their brothers, would disappear forever. By changing their future, the six men might never have been born.

As though he was thinking along the same lines, Four's arms tightened around her. His lips sifted through her hair as he pulled her close in a long, fervent hug that seemed almost desperate — almost as desperate as Sam felt.

The elevator doors opened suddenly and the party tumbled out of the crowded car. Deuce put a stumbling Jerri back on her feet before grasping her hand and towing her toward the lobby.

"You still haven't told us where the masks are hidden," Jerri pointed out, panting lightly as she tried to keep up with the determined men.

"Hidden?" Deuce exclaimed. "The masks aren't hidden!"

"They aren't? But, then… Well, where are they?"

"Right here in the lobby," Four answered for his brother. "Mr. Janus took a page from Edgar Allan Poe's *Purloined Letter*. Evidently, he decided his precious masks were best hidden in plain view."

"Plain view?" Sam argued as she clung to Four's hand. "But I've never seen them."

"Yes you have," he told her. "At least, you probably have. You just didn't realize what you were looking at."

They strode across the gleaming marble floors, swiftly approaching the wide, circular lake in the center of the glittering lobby. The water's polished surface shifted quietly, stretching and reshaping the golden reflection of the domed ceiling overhead. At the center of the lake, on its gilt surface, danced a little misshapen blob of silver. Four pointed out across the water. "What do you see?" he asked Sam as he strode toward the artificial lake.

Sam frowned at the water for a few seconds before her eyes opened wide. Her head snapped back as she stared upward into the lofty dome that arched over the expansive lobby. High overhead, a circle studded the very center of the curved ceiling. Within that distant circle gleamed two silver masks that fitted together so neatly, they looked like they were joined.

"Holy Moly," Sam murmured as she stared upward.

A flash of movement on the other side of the lake drew her gaze back down again. Across the water, she saw a tall man with raven hair streak toward a slender blonde woman. A woman who rose slowly into the air.

* * * * *

The casino's cavernous lobby filled with an excited rush of *oohs* and *ahhs* as a swarm of onlookers witnessed the young woman rising from the marble floor. All eyes turned toward the bizarre spectacle, unaware of the raven-haired man moving in a rapid blur across the gleaming marble floor toward her. Only Sam, Jerri and their four handsome companions noticed the strong, lithe figure racing to intercept what must have been the younger sister of the woman who'd robbed their booth. The girl, though bearing a remarkable likeness to her blonde sibling, had about her person a decidedly different air of innocence.

She'd just reached ten feet, her floral print skirt flapping softly against the smooth length of her thighs, smiling as she blew a playful kiss down at her cheering spectators, when the man leapt into the air, his dark, muscular body hurtling over the crowd in a beautiful, mesmerizing arc. Long arms wrapped around the woman's waist, securing her against his chest as he landed on the hard floor, his speed taking them into a fast, blurring roll.

The blonde screamed, the sharp sound muffled against his broad chest as he wrapped her in his arms and they tumbled across the slick marble in a flash of movement, long, dark limbs entwined around slim fair ones, raven hair tangled with platinum blonde. Lying on her back, the woman found herself trapped by the grinning man wedged between her indecently spread legs, holding himself on his arms above her.

"Are you out of your mind?" she wailed breathlessly, pushing against this chest but unable to budge him.

"That probably depends on who you ask," he drawled, not even winded from the miraculous leap that had taken her down.

"I think you broke my shoes!" she all but sobbed, the thick platform wedges no longer propelling air, now lying silent and still on her feet. "My sister is going to kill me!"

He ignored her about the shoes as well as the mention of a sister and leaned closer, nuzzling the side of her throat while catching her wrists and pressing her hands up above her head, pinning them to the cold hard marble beneath her back. "Mmm, I've never smelled a woman like you before," he murmured thickly.

She gasped a small, quiet sound of outrage. "I do not smell, you miserable ass!"

The brothers and Jerri and Sam finally fought their way through the growing crowd quickly gathering around the couple on the floor and immediately began asking people to move back. Five ignored them, keeping his attention on the blonde.

"I don't mean that you smell bad, darlin'. It's just…your scent is…" he murmured, shaking his head as he stroked his thumbs over the damp heat of her small, soft palms. "It's so—"

"Human," Kar'four grunted at his side, jabbing him in his ribs with the toe of one black leather boot. "Yeah, we get it, Five. She's flesh and blood and an evil little conniver to boot, so get off of her!"

"Yeah," she whispered, a strange, sudden shyness combining with the fire of anger and worry in her deep green eyes. "I think...I think it's time you got off of me."

"Son of a single port Synnie!" Ace muttered, his deep voice harsh with impatience, narrowed eyes searching the crowd from beneath the brim of his straw cowboy hat. "Where's the other blonde?"

Five jerked his head toward the water. "Sixpack followed her to the other side of the lake. He's probably already got her."

"Watch Sam for me," Kar'four growled at Deuce, taking off through the mass of people. Ace and Tré spread their attention between watching the dome, keeping an eye on Kar'five and the woman and controlling the thickening throng of spectators.

"You have to let me go," the blonde demanded in a whimper, struggling to break free of his hold. "Now!"

Five flashed her a devilish smile, rolling his hips against the vulnerable, intimate hollow between her thighs. "Why the rush? You haven't even given me a test drive yet."

For the brief flash of a moment, she stared up at him and her eyes went hazy, heat crawling up over her pale skin like a feverish mist, before she began bucking beneath his heavy weight, trying to throw him off. "You're going to get me killed!" she choked out.

"Now why would I want to go and do that, when you're so pretty?" he laughed softly, studying her with a lopsided smile. "Could be that I've just saved your life."

"Yeah, pretty and a killer," Deuce growled, keeping his voice low so as not to be overheard by the throng of hotel guests crowding in for a closer look. "You really know how to pick 'em, Five."

Taking a slow, deep breath, the woman quit struggling. "You've got two seconds to get off of me before I scream assault."

"Now see, here's the problem," Five murmured, leaning his dark face closer to hers. "I might look all cute and cuddly but don't let the good looks deceive you. I can be a real prick when it's called for." He slanted her a long, knowing look from beneath his lashes and flexed his hands against her wrists, just enough to allow the tips of his unsheathed claws to prick at her delicate flesh, before quickly drawing them back in. She gasped and her soft green eyes went wide with terror as she stared up at him.

"Oh my god," she whispered. "Wh-what are you?"

"Is it going to be called for?" he asked, his smile tight as he ignored her question. "Or are you going to play nice?"

"N-not in a m-million years," she stammered, the fear in her eyes too clear to miss.

He made a grating noise like a buzzer. "Wrong answer. Shall we try door number two? I can be a lot of fun to play with, honey, but I'm going to need your cooperation."

While Ace and Tré continued to move the crowd back, reassuring everyone that there was nothing wrong, other than a small technical deficiency in the merchandise, Deuce stared down at his brother and the blonde. "I don't fucking believe it," he snarled. "You're actually hitting on her? Now?"

Five shrugged, never taking the dark heat of his gaze off the woman. "You gotta admit, she *is* a babe."

"You can't keep her, Five," Deuce sighed, knowing where this was headed.

Broad shoulders lifted in another elegant shrug. "Why not?"

"For one," Deuce snorted, "she's pure evil."

"She's a thief," Five sighed, shifting off of her, while keeping her in his hold and pulling her gently to her feet. Even with the thick platforms on her tiny feet, she barely reached his shoulders. "But it's not like she's *planning* on destroying the world."

"What?" the blonde croaked, her dark green eyes going round at his words as she stared up at him. "Destroy the world? What the hell are you talking about?"

"For the love of the sun washed plains," Ace muttered over his shoulder, his arms spread wide as he continued to hold people back. "Can't you ever learn to keep your mouth shut? We've got a crowd problem here, in case it escaped your notice."

"It's his brains," Tré interjected, sending Five a brotherly look of pity.

Ace snorted. "You mean he doesn't have any?"

"Naw," Tré drawled as he gave his knitted cap a self-conscious tug. "They're just all in his dick."

"All I'm saying," Five argued, pulling the blonde, who appeared to be stunned into a quiet, paralyzed shock, against his chest, "is that we know she's bad but not necessarily evil."

Deuce curled his lip, a low, vibrating animal sound breaking out of his chest. "You know what?" he growled. "Tré's right! Your brains *are* in your dick!"

In an obvious attempt to change the subject, Five turned his attention to Jerri and Sam. "And who might these lovelies be?"

"They're mine and Kar'four's," Deuce barked, his dark expression daring Five to make an outrageous move.

"It's nice to meet you," Jerri said, blushing from the long, intimate look Five rolled from her toes to the top of her head.

"Trust me, sweetheart. The pleasure's all mine," he purred, sending the women a charming smile that revealed the very tips of his white fangs.

"Let me guess," Sam murmured to Deuce. "His host mother...was some kind of cat?"

"A leopard," Deuce sighed. "She was a leopard."

"And you know what they say," Five laughed, flashing the girls a mischievous grin.

"What's that?" Jerri asked a little breathlessly, making Deuce scowl.

Five secured the blonde at his side with his arm around her waist and reached for Jerri's hand, pressing a slow, lingering kiss to her palm, before straightening and shaking his hair away from his face. Jerri gasped as her eyes widened on the strange mottled spots that marked one side of his jaw and crawled down his neck, disappearing beneath the collar of his shirt, while Kar'five gave her a teasing wink. "We leopards never change our spots."

Before the husky words had finished leaving his lips, the blonde suddenly exploded into action, twisting and jabbing her elbow into his ribs at the same time that she rammed her knee into his groin. Air burst from his lungs in a choked cry of pain then his knees hit the floor hard as he doubled over. The others rushed forward but the crowd, eager to see what had happened, surged forward with them, tangling them up in a sea of curious spectators. Before anyone could reach her, the blonde tapped the toes of her shoes against the floor, hitting some kind of ignition switch and began swiftly rising into the air.

Struggling to his feet, his face red with pain and fury, Kar'five reached for her but without his running start, he couldn't jump high enough to grab hold, the tips of his long fingers just brushing at the flapping fabric of her skirt. As she floated away, she sent him a strange, solemn look, then turned and soared over the lake, her tattered skirt whipping against her legs, the soft fabric shredded from the lethal slice of his claws.

Chapter Fifteen
Sixty Seconds to Disaster

ഇ

"Son of a dickless clone," Five growled in male outrage, watching in fury as the pretty Synnie look-alike moved higher and higher. "She fucking kneed me in the balls!"

"Balls my ass," Deuce growled, glaring at his brother. "Tré was right! She crammed her knee into your damn brains!"

As the blonde rose over the water, an enthusiastic wave of applause broke from the crowd of spectators who now ringed the perimeter of the lake. More people hurried across the huge lobby to join the clapping audience.

Jerri stared at the faces around her, shaking her head in wry disbelief. The crowd forming around the artificial lake obviously thought they were watching a performance staged for their entertainment. She scanned the mob of spectators, trying to locate Kar'four. She found him on the other side of the water, moving swiftly at the crowd's edge, trying to find and run down the second blonde thief.

As Jerri pulled her gaze back over the crowd, her eyes snagged on a platinum head of hair framing a malevolent face. The woman's blue eyes were fixed on her sister hovering twenty feet above the lake and waving to the crowd below. With an impatient expression twisting her red-painted lips, the blonde in the crowd lifted her wrist and frowned at her watch.

"Deuce," Jerri murmured, nudging him in the ribs. "Look!"

Deuce followed her gaze across the lake. His brilliant eyes narrowed as he flicked his gaze to the back of the crowd, searching for his brother. "Four!" he shouted as his brother moved at the edge of the mob, still searching for the second blonde thief.

"He can't hear you," Jerri warned him.

Deuce took a deep breath. The next sound that issued from his lips was a low frequency hum followed by a riffle of deep notes.

On the other side of the lake, his brother stopped. Four's eyes moved swiftly to Deuce's face then homed in on their platinum-haired target.

At almost the same instant, the audience gasped. Jerri's attention was whipped back to the figure floating above the lake. The hovering blonde dropped suddenly as the jets on her shoes cut out, sputtered back to life for a few seconds then died. She plummeted twenty feet and entered the water with a scream and a splash, the weight of the jet shoes pulling her under as she struggled to stay afloat.

Jerri's gaze cut quickly back to the older sister in the crowd just in time to catch the wicked smile that curved the woman's red lips. The bitch had planned her own sister's demise! Stunned, Jerri shook her head again, hardly noting that Deuce had left her side. After kicking his shoes off at the edge of the indoor lake, he cut a smooth dive into the water. But not before his brother, Five, hit the water with a splash. Together, both brothers sliced through the water toward the sinking blonde. On the opposite side of the lake, Kar'four pushed his way through the pack of onlookers, fighting his way toward the older sister.

He was reaching for the bitch's shoulder when she shot into the air.

"I *really* should have kicked her scrawny ass when I had the chance," Sam growled at Jerri's side as they watched the woman lift above the crowd. It was obvious that the shoes this blonde wore were far more powerful, and probably a good deal more reliable, than her sister's pair. She slashed upward like a rocket out of a bottle, soaring to the dome's ceiling in a matter of seconds. She'd snatched the mercoldium masks from the dome's center before Kar'four even had his shirt off. Down on the casino floor, hemmed in by the people who stared up at the sight of a second flying female, Kar'four struggled to change into his bat form. He shook out his arms as he leapt upward, his wings forming in midair as he lifted away from the ground.

"Holy shit!" someone called out from the crowd, while everyone pointed and stared at the bizarre sight of a man flying...with wings!

"He must be part of the show!" another spectator shouted in a thick Texan drawl. "Don't you just love New Las Vegas?"

By this time, the blonde thief was halfway across the other side of the lobby, her stolen treasure clutched to her chest as she descended gracefully toward the floor.

Again applause rang out, the crowd convinced they were watching a promotional attraction rather than witnessing what was shaping up to be the end of the world.

"Oh my god. We're too late," Sam gasped, clutching at her best friend's hand with an icy grip.

Jerri's heart dropped as she tightened her hold on Sam's cool fingers. Sixty seconds to disaster. According to what Deuce and Four had told them, sixty seconds after the removal of the masks, the Casino's automated security system would release its deadly gas.

Faced with the prospect of death within ten days, Jerri turned her mind from the terrifying reality of the idea. Instead, she fixated on the masks. How on earth was the blonde able to remove them so swiftly? The damned things were mounted flush with the ceiling! They'd have to have been screwed in, nailed in or recessed beneath a frame to prevent them from falling to the ground.

Wouldn't they?

They couldn't just...cling to the ceiling.

Jerri's eyes narrowed. *Or could they?* Jerri knew of at least one other material that acted in that very same manner, defying gravity and clinging to a vertical surface without falling—the masks that molded themselves to their lovers' faces.

"I'm going to kill him," she muttered heatedly under her breath.

While Jerri's thoughts spun, she was distantly aware of Sam murmuring, "It's not their fault, Jerri. They've done the best they could."

"They're wearing mercoldium masks, Sam! Four and Deuce! Those masks on their faces are either copies of the stolen masks or the original masks themselves—brought back through time to be returned to the Palace." Jerri growled out loud. "Sam! They have a back up plan and we weren't in on it!" Again she growled. *If* they somehow managed to succeed in saving the day and *if* Deuce didn't evaporate immediately afterward, the man was in for a reaming! Her angry gaze burned at her lover as he pulled himself out of the lake, then reached down to help Five get his blonde out of the water.

Meanwhile, Kar'four had left the older blonde striding toward the casino exit, her stolen booty in hand, while he flapped back toward his brother. A note that sounded suspiciously like sonar warned Four's brother of his approach and Deuce turned to face his flying twin, peeling his mask from his face and holding it up for Kar'four to snag in the thick claw-like thumb that sprang from the joint folding his wing midspan.

With Deuce's mask in hand, Four beat his way back up to the ceiling and slapped it into place.

Fifty seconds to go.

Pulling his own mask away from his face, Four lifted it. At the same time, a male voice rang out, followed by the sharp retort of a gun. The vicious sound cracked and echoed in the domed ceiling as a ragged hole appeared in Four's wing.

The Casino's security personnel had finally reacted to the bizarre events unfolding beneath the lobby's domed ceiling, realizing that the priceless mercoldium masks were under threat. Two uniformed men stood just inside the lobby's entrance, their guns drawn. But while the real thief schmoozed through the exit doors unchallenged, the security guards were shooting at the winged man who was trying to thwart the robbery and return the masks to their station above the lake.

At Jerri's side, Sam screamed.

The rent in Four's wing widened as he beat at the air. He dropped toward the water, flapping vainly, striving hopelessly to lift himself back to the ceiling. The second mask glimmered in his claw-like thumb, descending with him as he fell toward the gleaming surface of the lake...with only forty seconds remaining before the security lights came on and the gas was released throughout the casino.

Sam heard a bellow of rage coming from her left and tried to focus but it was difficult to get past the panic of seeing the man she loved shot out of the sky! She felt frozen, locked down, while everyone around her exploded into action.

"Sam, look!" Jerri cried, pulling her arm with a violent yank and she turned to see Ace flashing through the crowd and tackling the armed guard at the knees. The man went down with a heavy thunk, his firearm jumping from his hand and spinning across the marble floor. Tré was right behind his brother, snarling as he hurtled toward a second security officer.

At the same time, Deuce dove into the lake and disappeared beneath its dark surface. Seconds later he appeared in the water beside his brother. Four's wings spread out on the surface of the water as his brother towed him back to the pool's edge.

Suddenly, her heart began to beat again and she gave herself a hard mental shake, knowing that she needed to think.

Thirty seconds to go.

After all the planning and maneuvering and six gorgeous studs sent back in time to preserve the future of womankind, it appeared as though she and Jerri were going to have to step in to save the world from disaster. Okay, they could handle it. She just needed to take a deep breath…and pray like hell that Jerri had a plan, because she was drawing a total blank. *Damn it*!

"Four is down," Jerri said, stating the obvious. "He can't fly," she added as her gaze swung to the dripping wet blonde standing beside Five at the edge of the indoor lake.

Sam followed Jerri's gaze down to the blonde's feet where she tottered on her thick wedges.

"I'm afraid of heights," Jerri went on to point out. "On the other hand, you can't swim worth a damn."

"What are you trying to tell me?" Sam muttered, not much liking the way this plan was shaping up.

"I'll get the mask," Jerri volunteered grimly. "You get the shoes."

"*I get the shoes*?" Sam squealed. "What kind of a plan is *that*? I might not be afraid of heights but that doesn't mean I can *fly*!" she shouted but by that time, Jerri was in the water, swimming toward Four and Deuce. With a belated curse, Sam sprang into action.

Ten seconds later, Jerri had intercepted the men as they splashed their way toward her. Ten seconds after that, she'd returned, gasping, to the edge of the pool. By that time, Sam had stripped the blonde of her elevator shoes. She was standing at the edge of the water, her arm outstretched like a relay runner reaching for the baton, waiting for Jerri to slap the mercoldium mask into her palm.

With the mask in her hand, Sam looked up into the casino lobby's lofty dome. She swallowed hard and tried to ignore her wobbly knees.

Ten seconds to go and one shot to get it right. After that was accomplished, she could take the time to have a total meltdown, if she still felt like it, complete with crying and screaming and whatever else the situation called for.

She tapped her toe against the ground and groaned when nothing happened. "Oh no you don't," she snarled. "I am *not* going to die because of some worthless pair of ugly-ass shoes!" With a rising feeling of panic and furious determination, she tapped her other toe. Immediately, she shot into the air — and smashed her head on the domed ceiling.

"Damn it!" she shouted, blinking away the stars that danced at the periphery of her vision. The air jets on the shoes continued to drive her head and shoulders against the ceiling, forcing her gradually, inexorably — and very fortunately — toward the center of the dome. When she reached the apex, Sam reached out with one hand and slapped Kar'four's mask beside its mate. As she watched, the mercoldium mask flowed into the empty space, filling it out to its edges.

How many seconds to go? By now, Sam had lost count. But the good news was that the lights hadn't come on throughout the Palace, which meant the casino security system hadn't been activated. At least, not yet. Sam gritted her teeth, choking on a litany of stinging curses while the shoe's jets continued to crush her head and shoulders into the dome's center. Seconds passed. Nothing happened. The lights didn't come on. No gas filled the casino.

And just as good as that was the fact that nobody shot at her.

Evidently, they'd succeeded in averting disaster. The masks had been returned to their places before the automated security system released the dangerous gas.

Sam blew out a crushing sigh of relief as she swiveled her head and peered down at the crowd. Below her on one side, Jerri jumped and clapped as she grinned up at her. Deuce knelt beside her best friend, an arm around Kar'four's shoulders. Four smiled up at her and she gave him a wink as she wondered how long the jets would last and how much longer she'd be pinned against the ceiling. She was about to shout a question down to the thief's sister when she caught a flash of activity at the casino's glass exit doors.

Sam laughed out loud.

There, just outside the casino's sliding glass doors, the unfortunate red-lipped thief had run into a very persistent young man who now held her firmly by the elbow. Though she pulled and struggled, the determined man with the dirty blonde hair would *not* let her go, aggressively demanding the return of his belongings.

Apparently the blonde thief had ripped off one too many people when she'd stolen the male prostitute's clothing.

And the cowboy wasn't having it.

Then the jets cut out. For a moment Sam hung on the silent air then she screamed as she dropped. She *really* couldn't swim worth a damn.

Chapter Sixteen
Cold Feet

Immediately after hitting the shimmering surface of the water, Sam began to thrash, the drenched denim of her jeans, as well as the heavy shoes, weighing her down. Her head dipped beneath the water's surface and a panic unlike anything she'd ever known surged through her system. She kicked like a mad woman, breaking the surface once again and her heart constricted with a sharp jolt of pain when she heard Four's hoarse shout.

"Get the fuck off me!" he snarled, his voice cracking with emotion. "She's drowning! I have to get to her!"

"You'll both drown if you get back in the water in your shape!" Deuce shouted back. "Five almost has her, Four. Stop fighting me and just look, damn it!"

Sure enough, in the next moment Sam felt a strong pair of arms wrap around her middle. Five's long legs kicked out beneath hers as he sidestroked through the water, pulling her toward the edge of the lake. She blinked with surprise to see not only Jerri, Deuce and Four but the younger blonde there as well, helping to pull her out. Before she could even draw a deep breath, Four was checking her soaked body with a trembling tenderness that made her smile.

"Hey," she tried to whisper but the noise from the cheering crowd, who still believed they were watching a show, drowned out the quiet word. "Hey," she said louder, reaching up one chilled hand to cup his cheek, waiting until his beautiful, terror-filled eyes met her gaze. "I'm okay, Four. I'm fine."

"I swear you scared ten years off me," he growled, pulling her into a tight, bone-crushing embrace. Behind her, she heard Deuce say, "We need to get the hell out of here, guys. While the crowd is still crazy and we *might* be able to sneak away in all the confusion."

"I can't believe you're still here," Jerri said in a soft rush, her voice hitching as she turned bright eyes up at the man holding her close, the searing heat in his gaze promising her untold pleasures as soon as he had her alone. "I can't believe you're *all* still here."

"Are they? All of them?" Sam asked, frowning anxiously. Other than Four and Deuce, only Five stood with them at the edge of the lake. "Where are the others?"

"Ace and Tré are dealing with the security guards," Four told her.

"And Sixpack has gone to make sure the cowboy doesn't need any help with this one's sister," Five said, one powerful arm banded about the shoulders of the younger blonde, as if to keep her from slipping away.

"We'd better disappear as quickly as possible," Deuce muttered, already pulling Jerri along with him as he set off through the crowd of spectators. They reached the elevators just as a set of doors were opening. All three couples shuffled in, then Deuce quickly hit the close button. As soon as they were on their way up, everyone sent the blonde and Five curious looks.

"She's with me," Five said simply, flashing a sharp, cat-like smile.

"I'm sticking around until I g-get some answers," the blonde stammered, managing to look confused and worried and fascinated all at once. "I want to know what my sister was up to."

"What did you think she was up to?" Kar'four asked, his long wings wrapped around Sam's drenched form, holding her so that her back was plastered to his front.

"Oh...um..." Her wide eyes seemed glued to the stunning sight of Four's wings but she finally managed to pull them away, settling her gaze on the gleaming floor of the elevator. She took a deep breath then slowly let it out. "Elevator shoes. We went into business together. She told me that if we could stage a really great promotional exhibit here at the Janus, our sales would take off. I sank every penny of my savings into her designs for those stupid shoes. No way was I going to let *him* destroy what we had planned," she huffed, glaring up at Five, who just kept grinning down at her like a jackass.

"And what exactly did you have planned?"

The blonde lifted one shoulder, her pale cheeks turning pink as she said, "I was supposed to float over the water...and...perform."

"Perform what?" Five asked, looking intrigued.

"A dance," she mumbled, her face turning pinker by the second.

His dark brows lifted in surprise. "You're a dancer?"

She nodded, tucking her hair behind her ears in a shy gesture. "I used to perform on the Old Broadway in New York, until my sister asked me to come to New Las Vegas a few months ago. She said she needed a partner to help her get her new business off the ground and, like a fool, I trusted her.

"She really did lie to me, didn't she?" the girl muttered, sounding pathetically miserable. "About all of it being a promotional stunt for our line of shoes."

"Yeah she did," Five sighed. "She was trying to steal the casino's mercoldium masks and she almost drowned you doing it. When your shoes cut out and you fell out of the sky, she was flying north to get the masks. Those shoes didn't fail by accident," he advised her in a softly purring growl. "No offense, sweetheart but your sister is a real bitch."

She gave him a sad nod without bothering to disagree.

"So, what's your name?"

"Sydney," she answered, her voice low. "Sydney Nylund."

The three men shared an instant's stunned silence. "Did you say...Sydney?" Five asked while giving his brothers a meaningful look.

"That's right."

The next words Five muttered to himself were hard to make out but it sounded like the word 'kismet' was in there somewhere.

She gave him a curious look. "And you and your brothers? You're not from around here, are you? Are you some sort of...special agents?"

"You could say that," Five replied, his laugh husky, his smile wry.

The elevator pinged, doors silently pulling open and everyone filed out into the hallway.

"You have someplace to go?" Four asked, looking eager to get Sam alone.

"Yeah," Five assured him with the briefest of glances, before returning his attention to the blonde at his side. "You guys run along and have fun. I'll let you know when the others are back."

* * * * *

"Are you sure the door to Jerri's room is locked?" Sam asked a bit later, cuddling up on Four's chest, careful to avoid his bandaged arm. "I don't want Deuce waltzing in here while I'm undressed."

The lovers were lying in their bed, drenched with exhaustion, wearing smiles of carnal satisfaction and little else.

"It's locked," he rumbled on a low laugh. "Deuce won't be bothering us."

"What about Five?"

"If I know my brother, he's got his hands full with that little blonde at the moment."

"She's certainly beautiful."

"What?"

"You don't think he got the better deal, do you?" she asked softly.

"Honey, he can have all the women in the world. And he's welcome to them. I've got exactly what I want, what I need and nothing is taking you away from me."

Sam jumped when he hooked a cold foot behind one of her calves. "Are you sure your brothers will be okay?"

"Which brothers?" he murmured against her ear.

"The ones who were arrested."

Kar'four rolled onto his back. A faint frown creased his forehead as he stared at the ceiling. "They'll be all right."

Sam shifted onto her side. Propped up on one elbow, she gazed down at her lover's electric blue eyes. He still wore a mercoldium mask covering the upper right side of his face. Sixpack had retrieved the masks from Sydney's sister and smuggled them upstairs—along with the news that Ace and Tré had been arrested. He hadn't appeared very happy about the whole situation, growling out his short explanation before quickly leaving again.

"Are you sure?" Sam pressed him.

Four shrugged. "When you get right down to it, no crime was committed. And the casino's cameras don't reach high enough to cover the center of the dome. Anyone who reviews the security tapes won't be able to tell exactly what happened. Inasmuch as my brothers and I are all identical, they'll be uncertain as to how many men were involved and what your role was in the fracas. Not to mention the fact that Mr. Janus probably won't want the newsnets publishing the story that his casino was very nearly robbed. If he's smart, he'll have a serious little talk with his security personnel then send his manager down to the courthouse to explain to the police that it was all a publicity stunt."

"And if he doesn't?"

"There isn't an incarceration device that can hold Tré. He could dig his way out of a bank vault."

Sam gave him a questioning smile.

"His mother was a badger," Four filled in.

Sam's smile widened thoughtfully.

"And if they make Ace take that cowboy hat off," Four whistled, "the term 'bad hair day' is going to take on a whole new meaning for everyone down at the county courthouse."

"Why is that?" Sam asked, laughing. "What is your brother hiding beneath his hat?"

"Well," Kar'four drawled, "he's hiding a whole lot more than the white hair that Tré is hiding."

Sam leaned in to nip playfully at the corner of Four's smile. "C'mon. Give me a hint. What's Ace got that Tré hasn't got?"

Shifting his weight suddenly, Four rolled her beneath him, pinning her against the mattress. "Don't bite," he growled as he leaned toward her mouth and caught her bottom lip between his teeth. He bit her lip provocatively then licked the puffy, swollen edge of her mouth. "That's my job."

He resettled his weight on his forearms as he gazed down on her and finally answered her question—sort of. "His mother was a thoroughbred."

"He has a mane?" Sam squeaked.

"Sticks up about three inches," Kar'four snickered. "Even in a gale wind."

Sam giggled. "They'll just think it's a Mohawk or something."

Four shook his head and laughed. "They *might* think that. Until they send him to the showers and realize there's more than gel making it stick up."

"Ah." Sam chuckled, grinning up at him. "Tell me more about your brothers. I like hearing about your family."

"Naw, that's enough about my brothers for now," Kar'four growled jealously, grinding his hips into the puff of soft hair on her mound. Then he lowered his mouth to hers and surged deep into her body.

* * * * *

In the next room, behind the locked adjoining door, Deuce swept his tongue around the inside shell of Jerri's ear. "What's wrong?" he murmured.

"Nothing," she answered.

Deuce sighed. "You can't lie to me, Jerri."

Jerri squirmed a bit beneath him, causing him no end of pleasure. By the seas, there was nothing more wonderful than a wriggling woman caught beneath your weight.

"Why not?" she asked with a pout in her voice.

He gave her a soft smile. "Because I know you too well."

She made a sulky little moue. "Deuce. We've only known each other two days. There's no way you could — "

He wanted to shut her up with a kiss but he restrained the impulse and explained. "Animal instincts. Our senses are more finely-honed than those of a twenty-first century human. My brothers and I can tell a lot about a person's basic personality without them having uttered a word. Yesterday, we knew you girls wouldn't place that bet on the baseball game. And right now…I know you're lying."

"You didn't know I was lying when I said I liked bats," she pointed out, her pout deepening. Deuce couldn't resist. She was, after all, asking for it with her plump bottom lip sticking out like a doorsill. He gave her mouth a bit of teeth and growled out a low sound of satisfaction as she stiffened beneath his body, her back arching on the bed, her luscious soft frame bowing against his. "Are you questioning me?"

"Well," she panted. "You didn't."

"Fuck," he confessed, his voice rough with disgust. "I was in such a panic, I wasn't thinking straight."

"You're thinking straight now," she murmured as she reached between their bodies and gave his cock a firm squeeze.

He closed his eyes and emitted a low, rumbling hum, the deep, sexy sound half-whale, half-very-aroused-male. "And you're changing the subject."

"I wasn't lying," she sulked.

"No," he agreed. "But you weren't telling the truth, either."

Jerri groaned out a soft sound of exasperation. "And you're going to know every time I — "

"Every time," he assured her. "So what's bothering you, my adorable little land nymph?"

Jerri gave a soft snort of amusement at her lover's sweet endearment. "Are you sure the masks are okay?" she finally forced herself to ask, not really wanting to worry about the damn things but unable to set her mind completely at ease. "Are you *sure* they're okay, right now, down in the casino lobby?"

Deuce blinked in surprise. "Sixpack is watching them."

"Right now?"

"Of course, *right now*. You didn't think we'd leave them unguarded, did you?"

Jerri shifted her gaze from his accusing blue stare. "No, of course not," she muttered.

He nuzzled his mouth into the hollow at the base of her throat. "Liar," he growled.

Jerri stretched beneath him as he pressed his erection into her belly. "I'm glad your brothers turned up."

"They did make a handy diversion, didn't they?"

"Makes me wonder what you'd have done without them," she mused.

Deuce's face turned grim. "We would have stopped the robbery, one way or another." He sighed. "But you're right. We probably wouldn't be lying here right now. We might still be watching the masks. We *might* even be in jail, instead of my two brothers.

"We didn't know much about the theft but the plan was for Four to guard the air while I covered the water below the masks. We didn't know from what direction the thieves would strike. There was also the concern that, during the robbery attempt, the masks might fall into the water. Most people don't realize it but that lake is thirty feet deep, designed primarily to limit access to the masks and protect them from theft. But the lake is also meant to function as a temporary vault should the masks fall from the ceiling by accident or design. Unlike me, a human would need scuba gear to retrieve them. While all of my brothers are strong swimmers, I'm the only one who can dive deeply enough and hold my breath for that long."

"Which explains why you and Four were selected to stop the robbery," Jerri summarized. "You were best suited. But I'm curious about the rest of your brothers, especially Tré. What's he hiding beneath that cap he's got pulled down around his ears?"

Deuce snorted. "Just a couple of white streaks in his hair. He probably thinks they make him look old."

"White streaks!" Jerri's voice betrayed her interest. "You mean…like a *wolverine*?"

Again he snorted. "*You wish!*" He teased her with several seconds of silence. "More like a badger."

"Ohhhh," she said quietly as Deuce smiled at her disappointment. "And what about Sixpack? He seemed a bit growly when he brought the masks up here to you guys."

"His mother was a wolf."

"Are those long sideburns of his…permanent?"

174

"Those sideburns aren't even sideburns. They're fur."

"And what about Ace?"

But Deuce cut her off. "That's enough about my brothers," he rumbled belligerently.

"Jealous?" she prodded him with a smug smile.

When his teeth grazed her neck, she arched her breasts into his hard chest. She felt his breath wash over her skin as he made his way from her neck downward. His teeth rode over her nipple in a rough statement of possession. "What do I have to be jealous about?" he growled at her between passion-fired nips.

Jerri groaned as her back bowed and her nipples stabbed into his waiting mouth. "Nothing," she breathed.

"That's right," he told her. "And don't you forget it."

* * * * *

Later that afternoon, they received a phone call from the Health Department thanking the women for sharing their research and assuring them that the canisters would be condemned first thing in the morning. A delegation from their office would be meeting with Mr. Janus to explain why the canisters were being confiscated and destroyed.

As an amusing aside, Sam and Jerri were offered positions at the New Las Vegas Health department as soon as they'd completed their "Master's thesis" and entered the workforce.

As the afternoon turned into evening, the two couples dragged themselves from their beds and rejoined each other for some quiet conversation which was eventually interrupted by a now-familiar pounding on the door. When the door was answered, three handsome, dark-haired men stood on the other side. The incarcerated brothers had been freed! Ace and Tré were ushered in ahead of Sixpack—Six wearing a gruff scowl, Ace wearing his cowboy hat and Tré with his knitted cap still tugged down around his ears.

Sam got her first good look at Sixpack and she had to admit she liked what she saw. Although another identical brother, this one had a commanding presence that set him apart from the others. Like the rest of his siblings, he wore his thick hair a bit on the long side, the blunt ends sweeping his jaw and partially obscuring his long sideburns. He carried himself with an unruly grace, a predatory glint in his eyes and a hard confidence in his smile, all of which, put together, declared him a born ladies man just waiting to be hatched.

True to form, Tré swept Jerri into his arms the first chance he got, planting a kiss on her lips before she could protest and before Deuce could knock his head off. When he danced away from his brother, leaving Jerri in his brother's arms, she managed to separate him from his hat.

The somewhat flustered Tré blushed an endearing shade of pink while the women fussed and raved over the wide white streaks that tapered as they swept from his temples back toward his nape. With a lopsided grin and a shy duck of his head, he pocketed the knitted cap once and for all.

After explaining that Five had taken Sydney to collect her things from her sister's apartment, the men milled about the room, sharing their stories while Sam ordered dinner on the wall-mounted room service control panel. With a roomful of hungry man-animals to feed, the tab was astronomical. Her fingers shook as she waved her credit key over the scanner and held her breath.

The charges were rejected. There wasn't enough money left in her account to pay for the meal. "I'm sorry," she mumbled anxiously, sending Jerri a look of appeal.

But while Jerri fished through her purse, trying to locate her own credit key, Ace stepped forward and flashed a gleaming rainbow key at the panel on the wall.

Sam gasped. She'd never seen a rainbow key before. Only billionaires carried the rare, multicolored keys. She stared at Ace as though he'd grown a tail.

Ace answered her stare with a grin. "I hate to be the one to tell you, sweetheart, but these cheapskate lovers of yours have been holding out on you."

Four was quick to react, his expression both shocked and hurt while Deuce looked just plain angry. "We haven't been *holding* out," he growled, "we've just been too busy to *cash* out!"

"Wh-What do you mean?" Jerri asked hesitantly, frowning first at Sam then at her lover.

In answer, Deuce plunked himself down on the edge of the bed and pulled off first his shoes and then his socks. He paused a moment to wag his finger at her. "I don't want to hear anymore complaints about my cold feet," he told her, then plucked something away from the sole of one bare foot—something a warm, silver color that slowly reshaped itself as she watched, shortening on one side, lengthening on the other, flowing into the palm of his outstretched hand.

"Ohhhhh," Jerri breathed, reaching out with one finger and drawing it over the cool surface of the mercoldium metal. "It's beautiful."

Deuce nodded. "And it's worth a fortune here in the twenty-first century, though it's common enough in the twenty-third. Scientists found a way to inexpensively reproduce the element back in 2105. Everyone wears it in place of those...those...shoe things."

"Ohhh," Jerri uttered, her eyes wide.

"We got five hundred thousand an ounce at the Pawn shop," Ace informed them.

"Which means we'll be able to live off the millions we're walking on," Four added, fingering his mask possessively.

"That's right," Deuce agreed. "And we'll be able to keep our masks."

"So...you guys are rich," Sam said, eyeing the control panel on the wall. Slowly, she moved toward it and started punching buttons.

"We told you that earlier," Four murmured, following her to the wall and watching her curiously. "What are you doing?"

"Just changing the order a little."

"Tacos!" he sputtered. "Don't cancel the tacos!"

"Don't panic, big guy. I have something better in mind for you."

"What could be better than tacos and...and beer?" he argued swiftly, his face falling as she punched another button and changed their drink order.

"Oh, sweetheart. You have a lot to learn about the past. Does the word Champagne mean anything to you? Filet Mignon? Crab Louis? Beef Oscar?"

"Champagne?"

"Just relax, lover, and let Sam make it good for you."

Chapter Seventeen
Don't Make Me Wait

ಬಿ

"Do you know what I want to do now?" Jerri asked Deuce after they'd pushed the long train of empty food carts into the corridor and returned to their room. The night was late and they were finally alone again. Four and Sam had only just closed the door to their room. The rest of Deuce's brothers had departed a bit earlier, arguing the merits of beer versus champagne as they piled through the door out into the corridor.

His eyes darkened with interest at her husky tone. "What?"

Leaning toward him on her tiptoes, Jerri whispered into his ear. When she pulled back, giving him a shy smile, Deuce grabbed her hand and growled, "Come on, let's go."

It took some careful maneuvering to avoid casino security but twenty minutes later Deuce led her into the enclosed atrium that was connected to the casino lobby through an ornately tiled hallway. At the end of the hall stood a double set of intricately carved doors sporting the same key design that was used in their rooms. With a playful smile, Deuce pushed one of the doors open and pulled her into the steam-filled, jasmine scented room, the fragrant flowers blooming from oversized terracotta pots that lined the walls. The huge Olympic-sized swimming pool glittered like a jewel, as blue as Deuce's mesmerizing eyes, white swirls of steam rising from its surface like a dragon's breath. He tilted up her chin and with a soft gasp, Jerri found herself staring up at the starry magnificence of the desert sky through a ceiling made entirely of glass.

"It's beautiful," she breathed out softly. "I've never seen anything so perfect."

"I have," Deuce whispered in a silken rasp roughened by hunger as his arms closed around her from behind. His face lowered and he nuzzled the sensitive skin behind her ear, his mouth warm and soft and delicious. Jerri shivered, desire pooling thickly in her middle, making her burn. Without any direction from the hungry male at her back, she reached for the buttons on her jeans and popped the first one, then the second, slowly undoing them until the material sagged low on her hips. Deuce's hand slid possessively inside the waistband and pushed the denim down her thighs, along with her panties, until they pooled around her ankles. Kicking them aside, Jerri reached for the hem of her shirt and Deuce's hand settled against her stomach. As the shirt cleared her head, his hand lowered, sliding across her skin, over the soft tuft of curls on her mound, his long, strong fingers curling against the swollen cushion of her pussy. The provocative touch demanded nothing but her acceptance, her pleasure and she trembled in reaction, while her pulse quickened.

"I love how soft you are," he rasped in her ear, the silken fall of his hair tickling her bare shoulder as she slipped off her bra. "How tender and sweet. Your little cunt's more delicate than I could have ever imagined," he whispered, easing the blunt tip of his index finger between her folds and opening her. A dark, sexual sound of craving rumbled in his chest when he found her hot and wet. Curling his free arm around her waist to hold her steady, he rimmed the puffy edge of her vulva with his fingertips, the smooth flesh already drenched with cream. Growling, he said, "These hot little juices taste a thousand times better than I could have ever dreamed."

Her low, husky moan of arousal turned into a sharp cry of pleasure when he took one wet fingertip and rubbed the moisture into the thrumming, swollen bud of her clit. The sensation was so intense that it arched her back while chill bumps spread over her flesh like a brush fire.

"I love going down on you," he added huskily, nipping her tender lobe. "Love eating this hot little cunt, kissing this precious little clit."

Suddenly, Jerri turned in his arms, her hands reaching for the hem of his shirt. Breathless, she said, "Enough teasing! I want you. Right now."

He laughed huskily, the erotic sound dark and delicious, utterly male. "Oh, you'll get me, sweetheart. Every day for the rest of our lives."

Jerri lifted her face for his kiss but Deuce hoisted her into his arms and tossed her high into the air. She flew like a bird in flight, silently screaming then landed with a splash in the middle of the pool. When she came up, sputtering as she struggled to get her hair out of her eyes, he was nowhere to be seen. "Deuce?" she whispered, suddenly unnerved but then she saw his clothes lying beside hers on the side of the pool.

He was in the water with her.

Jerri stared into the water around her and below her but the ethereal streams of moonlight and softly muted pool lights were too dim to ease the shadows from the dark water there in the deep end of the swimming pool. The deep indigo blue of the tiles made it impossible to see what was beside her…underneath her. She was alone, drifting, and yet she knew Deuce was close as a sudden whoosh sped by her left side, the current changing in the water as something powerful moved through the warm pool, rapid and swift. He'd changed into his animal form, like she'd asked him to upstairs, and now he was circling her, hunting her, but she wasn't afraid. The warm, rich spill of desire ramping up her heart rate told her she wanted to be captured by him. Captured…and claimed.

Something brushed against her right leg and her breath caught, her arousal taking on a hard, urgent edge. She wondered if he could scent the warm juices slipping from her pussy into the water the way a shark could scent a drop of blood from miles away. Her teeth sank into her lower lip as she treaded water, turning in a slow circle as she tried to spot him, when strong fingers suddenly caught at her hips, supporting her weight and she felt the broad width of his powerful shoulders pressing between her legs, pushing them apart.

Shaking with soft, almost silent giggles of excitement, Jerri allowed her legs to drift apart and it was unbearably erotic, the warm lap of the water against her soft, tender parts. Underwater, Deuce brushed a gentle kiss against her navel, then lower, nuzzling the wet curls on her mound. His hands clutched at her soft thighs, fingers digging into her flesh and Jerri felt her weight being levered higher in the water. His thumbs found the swollen outer lips of her pussy and pulled them apart so that her clit popped out, shamelessly begging for his attention. Then his tongue flicked out, lapping against her screamingly sensitive clit, and she bit her lip so hard that she tasted blood. As if sensing just how to unravel her, Deuce suckled the throbbing little pulse of pleasure, then licked his way to the tiny opening and thrust his tongue into her, the eager movements of his mouth telling her without words how much he loved what he was doing.

Jerri thrashed in the water, head flung back as she stared sightlessly at the shimmering canopy of the stars, her entire being focused on the heavy pulse of pleasure beating between her legs. He kept the delicious tongue-fuck going until she was sobbing, breathless, then closed his lips around her clit once again and pushed two big fingers into her pussy, hooking them forward. She went over, flying, the pleasure convulsing through her, radiating from her core until it pulsed in her fingertips and toes. Jerri let her upper body fall back to the surface of the water, arms flung wide as she simply enjoyed the dark, endless rush of ecstasy that rolled through her like waves surging across the deepest ocean.

Stroking deep with his tongue, Deuce couldn't get enough of Jerri's devastating taste. It was too good, salty and sweet, completely addictive. He'd have happily kept his tongue buried in that delicious, clutching cunt all night long but his cock had demands of its own. Unfortunately, he didn't know how the fearless little human was going to feel about meeting them.

Better hope she doesn't run screaming in the other direction.

Though he had shed his shirt and allowed his animal DNA to transform his human shape, Jerri had yet to see all of him in the raw while he was in his altered form. He'd already retaken his human shape when they'd made love the night before, so she hadn't seen his cock when it was...*different.*

Hunger was driving him to move hard and fast—but he had to at least warn her about what was coming. Had to make sure her body was as wet and soft as possible, before he buried himself in that exquisitely sweet pussy. Grasping her hips, Deuce kicked his legs and powered their bodies through the warm water until they'd reached the middle of the pool, where he could firmly touch the bottom. He broke the surface of the water and Jerri lifted her head, giving him a sweet, tender smile that made his chest hurt, he loved her so much.

"I want you, Deuce. Please don't make me wait any longer."

"Jerri," he said tightly, swallowing against his worry and fear. He knew she accepted him without judgment but he couldn't help the small kernel of doubt that she would be scared of him...like this. "Honey, I need...need to tell you something."

"Tell me later," she murmured, pushing her wet bangs back from her smooth forehead, her brown eyes bright with desire. "Right now, all I can think about is how badly I want you inside me. Please, Deuce."

"Jerri...damn it, I have to tell you. This isn't going to be like it was...before."

She cocked her head to the side as she waited for him to explain, a small half smile playing at her beautiful mouth, as if she thought he was being playful, teasing her.

Taking a deep breath, Deuce grabbed her small hand and carried it down his body, curling her fingers around his cock. She gasped, her big brown eyes going instantly wide with shock. "*Oh my god,*" she said hoarsely.

"I know," he groaned, trembling from the feel of her soft fingers against his rigid, heavily veined shaft. "That's what I was trying to tell you. My arms and chest aren't the only things that get...*thicker* when I'm in this form. Do you want...do you want me to change back before we...before I—"

"No," she said in a small, breathy voice, stroking him with a tender, inquisitive touch that was driving him to the dangerous edge of madness. Her eyes went hazy, lips parted for her slow, deep breaths. "No...I want you like this, Deuce. I want all of you, all of this," she whispered, tightening her hand against his thickness, "buried deep inside me."

"It won't be easy if I fuck you like this, Jerri. I'm too turned on and too bloody big."

The corner of her mouth twitched. "Who said I want easy? My life hasn't been easy since the second I set eyes on you and you know what? I wouldn't have it any other way, Deuce."

He pressed his forehead to hers, his voice ragged with need, thick with excitement. "I could hurt you."

"But you won't," she said gently, taking his other hand and moving it between her legs. "Feel me, Deuce. I'm soaked. Drenched. You'll have to be careful at first but I can...I can take you. I was made to take you."

With her hand gripping his cock just under the fat, bulbous head, she drifted closer to his body, until she could stroke the sensitive crown through the puffy folds of her cunt. Even in the water, he could feel her slippery juices slicking across the sensitive head, making him grind his jaw, it felt so fucking good. "Come on, Deuce," she teased, leaning forward to nip the side of his throat, making him jump in her hold. "Give me what I want. Give me *you.*"

"Jerri," he growled, shoving her through the water until they came up against the side of the pool, her back plastered to the warm blue tiles. Gritting his teeth, he struggled for control but the second he had her in place, he pressed forward, pushing the heavy head of his cock into her. She was exquisitely tight and small and he was impossibly thick. Cushiony softness surrounded him, clamped down on him like a silken vise, as he pressed inward in small, restrained lunges, terrified he was going to hurt her. "Are you okay? Is it too much?"

"Feels incredible," she panted, her breath warm against the side of his throat.

"You want more?" he grunted, swallowing, shaking from the effort it took to hold himself in check, to keep from shoving himself into her.

"God, yes. All of you. Don't you dare hold back on me."

He pressed her more firmly against the side of the pool and dug his fingers into the tiled lip hard enough to crack it. Her thighs lifted higher around his hips and he thrust into her, giving her another thick inch, stretching the tight, lush depths of her sex. She felt so good, so hot and wet and soft, he had to bite the inside of his cheek to keep from shouting out his pleasure and alerting the security staff to their presence.

"Tell me if I hurt you," he demanded, his voice guttural, raw.

"If you don't hurry up and fuck me," she panted, "*I'm* going to hurt *you*."

A low, hoarse laugh vibrated deep in his chest and he arched his back, lowering his head until he could touch the tip of his tongue to one of those sweet, berry-red nipples. "I'm going to fuck you," he growled against the sweet tip, staring up at her through his lashes. "I'm going to fuck you so hard that we have to crawl back up to the room. I just have to get my damn dick in you first and I *do not want to hurt you*."

"You won't," she promised. "You won't."

Pressing the pad of his thumb to her clit, he shuddered as more of that sweet, honeyed cream gushed around him, easing his way. "God, you get so wet when I do that. I wonder how wet you'll get when I do this?" he murmured, smiling wickedly as he slid his fingers back between the smooth cheeks of her bottom, until he was rubbing against the puckered entrance nestled there between the soft globes.

"Deuce?" she gasped and he knew that he'd shocked her with the carnal caress.

Breathing the words into the sensitive shell of her ear, he said, "There's no part of you that I don't love, Jerri. That I don't want to claim as mine and mine alone."

He pushed the tip of one finger past the tight ring of muscle and her cunt spasmed in reaction, making them both groan from the breathtaking sensation.

"Mmm, you like this," he rasped, so turned on he could barely get his voice to work. "I can feel your little pussy getting wetter, hotter, slicker." He fingered her ass while he sank his cock another inch into her perfect little cunt, then another. His lips pulled back over his teeth as he hissed from the devastating pleasure. "God that feels good."

He set up a rhythm then, fingering her backside as he inched the massive bulk of his cock into her, while she hid her face in the crook of his shoulder, her breaths hot and fast against his skin, nails digging into his biceps as she held onto him, the soft, erotic cries spilling from her throat making him so hot, he was surprised steam didn't come out his ears.

When he was finally buried all the way inside, Deuce speared the fingers of his free hand into the wet strands of her hair and cupped the back of her head in his palm. "Look at me," he demanded in a dark, rough voice, filled with equal parts tenderness and hard, savage hunger. He wanted to pound into her, driving his cock hard and deep again and again, but knew he needed to give her sweet little pussy time to get used to the size of him. He was big even in his human form — and like *this* — hell, it still amazed him that she was able to take him. But then, he knew, in his heart, that this precious little human was truly made for him. Every sweet, breathtaking, heart-warming inch of her. "I want to know everything about you," he growled, the fierce sense of possessiveness burning through his veins more powerful than anything he'd ever known. "I want to spend the rest of my life learning everything there is to know, Jerri."

"There isn't much," she admitted wryly, her mouth twisting, face flushed and passion-damp. "I'm just...just your average, All-American girl. What you see is what you get."

"Good," he growled, sending the finger in her ass a little deeper, until she gave a low, throaty purr of pleasure. "Good," he repeated. "Because I *love* what I see. I love everything about you."

Deuce noticed that the color in her cheeks darkened every time he used the L word. He wanted to tell her everything that was in his heart—his very soul—but he and Four had decided to tell them in the morning, to make it special.

"Really?" she asked softly.

"Yeah really. And you're crazy if you think there's anything average about you. You're an amazing woman, Jerri. Warm and tender, hot and lush. Giving and selfless, strong and courageous. I'm lucky as hell that I caught you before some asshole could steal you up for his own."

Her lashes fluttered and she flicked her tongue against the pink swell of her lower lip. "Is that what you're going to do, Deuce? Steal me up?"

"Damn straight. I'm going to fuck you and fill you up with cum and god help the bastard who ever tries to take you away from me." He pulled her face close and pressed a tender kiss to her mouth, then whispered, "Now hold onto me because this is gonna be a hell of a finish, sweetheart."

Jerri's breath caught as Deuce pulled those thick, immense inches of cock out of her pussy, inch by inch, then drove them deliciously back into her, jerking a husky cry right out of her throat. The finger he'd pressed into her backside stroked the thin membrane that separated the long digit from his cock as his pelvis ground against the swollen bud of her clit. Her back arched as pleasure suffused her body in a heavy, relentless stream that all but blocked out reality. All she knew was the feel of him buried so powerfully inside her, stretching her, stroking tender, forbidden places that made her pussy cream around him, easing the way for that massive cock that kept pulling back and lunging harder, deeper, until she was biting her lip again as she tried to hold in the screams of pleasure breaking out of her.

There was no slow, steady build to orgasm. It hit her like a flash of lightning—hard and hot and brilliant—holding her in its grip as the sensations speared through her in ever-widening circles, permeating every inch of her body. Her sheath convulsed around his hard flesh and he growled a dark, primal sound of carnal satisfaction in her ear, pinning her to the wall as his own orgasm tore through him. Jerri felt the power of him pour into her, his hot cum surging into her with stunning force, jerking from the thick head he had jammed against the mouth of her womb, filling her up.

They clung like that, to the side of the pool, for what seemed like an endless eternity, shuddering and shaking as the pleasure slowly eased, until they could once again breath. Jerri blinked the tears from her eyes, unsurprised to realize she'd cried. The experience had been too emotional, too powerful, to hold inside.

Deuce pulled his finger from her body and stroked his palm against the silky skin of her bottom, waiting until his cock had finally softened before pulling himself out of her. She gasped at the startling sensation and he pressed his lips to her ear. "Are you okay?" he asked, his voice tender with concern.

She patted his shoulder. "Perfect," she said sleepily, feeling wrung out and completely boneless. He snuffled a soft laugh against the side of her throat at the slurred sound of satisfaction in that single word and she somehow found the energy to give a soft, happy giggle in return.

"Just close your eyes and rest," he murmured, taking her in his strong arms and holding her against his chest as the warm water lapped against them. "I've got you, baby."

With a soft smile playing at her lips, Jerri closed her eyes and drifted away into satisfied slumber.

Chapter Eighteen
Is This the End?

ော

The next morning, Sam stretched languorously in the middle of the bed, reviewing the events of the preceding day. All in all, a good one, she decided. They'd saved the world, discovered that their lovers were filthy rich and—best of all—the men hadn't disappeared after they'd stopped the theft and changed their future.

She let out a nice long, satisfied sigh. Her well-used body ached deliciously in all the right places as she wiggled her toes and squeezed her hands into tight, round fists. Reaching behind her to plump up her pillow and glancing at the open door that led to Jerri's room, she wondered vaguely where her lover had gotten to.

Her lazy smile was smug as she turned her head and gazed at the clock on the bedside table. Slowly, her smile faltered as her toes turned cold. The clock read eleven-thirty. Sam's heart stopped. The robbery—the original robbery—was to have taken place between ten and eleven on July twenty-fifth. If the men were going to disappear because of the changes they'd made to their own future, they would disappear at the *exact* time of the *original* robbery.

It was July twenty-fifth. It was almost noon. And Sam had been sleeping when the clock ticked its way from ten to eleven.

Sam tried to draw in a breath but her lungs felt as though they were compressed around her heart. *Kar'four was nowhere to be seen.* She reached for the empty space, rubbing her hand across the vacant sheets where Four should have been lying beside her. The sheets were cool to her grasping touch.

Kar'four was gone.

"Jerri!" she wailed, tearing at the sheets and wrapping herself up in lacey eyelet as she rushed toward the open door connecting their rooms. "Jerri, they're gone!"

* * * * *

Four and Deuce paused on the other side of Sam's hotel room door, while Deuce dug in the front pocket of his jeans and pulled out a small velvet box. "Are you sure this is the way to do it?" he whispered.

Kar'four gave him a brief nod. "Diamond rings. Almost all of the romantic archives mentioned diamond rings when it came time to wrap up the relationship."

Deuce swiped with one hand at the tiny beads of sweat speckling his upper lip. "And...you reckon it would be all right for us to...to tell them we love them at this point?"

Four seemed a little less certain on this matter. "I *think* so." He closed his eyes and searched his mind. "The hero always tells the heroine that he loves her at the *end* of the story."

"Is this the end of the story?" Deuce asked nervously.

Four screwed his lips into a thoughtful knot. "I think it must be. I mean, we stopped the robbery and saved womankind. Sounds like some kind of ending to me. In fact, it sounds like a damn happy ending."

"Right," Deuce said anxiously. "Right." Lifting the box top, he squinted at the bright bit of jewelry in the dark case. "And you're sure those look like waves?" he asked his brother.

"Yes," Four reassured him for the umpteenth time. After purchasing the diamond engagement rings, the brothers had molded bits of their priceless mercoldium on either side of the glittering stones, adding their own personal touch to each ring.

Glancing curiously at Four's box, he asked, "What did you put on yours? A bat?"

Four grimaced. "I went with wings. Thought they'd be more romantic."

Deuce sent him a nervous grin. "Don't worry. Sam will love it."

"So," Kar'four reviewed for his brother's sake, "we walk in, surprise them with these...engagement rings...and make plans for a honeymoon on some tropical island."

"Good." Deuce answered. "Good. Just as long as it isn't Tahiti."

Kar'four gave him a sharp look. "Why not Tahiti?"

"Because of the hurricane."

"Hurricane?"

"August seventeenth, 2050," Deuce informed him distractedly.

"Oh," Kar'four said, slowly nodding his understanding. "Right." He smiled suddenly. "Glad I brought you along."

Deuce gave him a wan smile and took a deep breath, motioning to his brother that he was ready. With that signal, Four waved his key at the door. Together the two brothers tiptoed into Sam's room.

The room was empty but Four could hear some light snuffling noises coming from the door that adjoined the two hotel rooms. The brothers shared a curious look and then, with a finger on his lips, Four warned his brother to be silent as they whipped out their diamond rings, popped the lids open and crept toward the open doorway.

After giving Deuce a bracing glance, Four stepped with his brother through the opening and shouted, "*Surprise!*" And after that, they had to move very quickly indeed, catching the women before they hit the floor.

Because Sam and Jerri had fainted dead away.

* * * * *

After Deuce and Four had revived the girls and popped the question, they celebrated their engagements by making love to their new fiancées. With that out of the way, they called their brothers and invited them back to Sam's room for champagne toasts.

While waiting for their brothers, Deuce tried to get Jerri to explain why they'd found the two women in tears earlier. "You'll think we are silly," Jerri hedged, hanging on to him as though she was afraid he might evaporate at any moment. Lifting her face, she searched his eyes. "You *are* here...for good, Deuce? You aren't going to disappear on me?"

His gaze softened as he looked down on her. "Oh, sweetheart. Please set your mind at ease. It's over. If we were going to disappear it would have happened at the time of the original robbery, when we changed our future."

"Then," she ventured sadly, "everything's gone? Your future doesn't exist anymore? And all the people you knew..."

"Were never born," he finished solemnly.

"But how can you be here, if you were never born?"

He shook his head. "I don't know. Any theories we could come up with would be just that—theories. We were somehow 'preserved' in this time. Even though we were born in a time that no longer exists, it existed when we left it to come here. It was real. We were real when we came here and though that future is now cut off from us, we're still real and we're still here." He stopped and checked her face. "Does any of that make any sense?"

"You aren't going to disappear," she murmured, as a knee-weakening feeling of relief washed over her tautly strung nerves. "That makes perfect sense—the most beautifully perfect sense I've ever heard."

Amidst the boisterous congratulations and good-natured ribbing that started up the minute the rest of the brothers trooped into their hotel rooms, Jerri pulled Sam, Deuce and Kar'four into a corner on the far side of the room. Speaking loud enough to be heard over the others, she said, "I meant to ask earlier about Sydney's sister."

"Taken care of," Deuce told her, slanting a look toward the quiet couple sitting in front of the mahogany desk. Five sprawled in the desk chair, unable to keep his eyes off a softly smiling Sydney, who sat in a matching chair that had been pulled in from the other room. It was obvious Five wanted her attention and equally obvious that the shy blonde was doing her best to ignore him.

"What do you *mean*, taken care of?" Sam demanded, pulling his attention away from the pair, her green eyes lit with a stubborn fire. "That blonde bitch deserves to pay for what she did to Sydney and for what she almost did to the *world*."

Deuce shrugged. "Got that covered."

Sam's eyes narrowed on him as she crossed her arms over her large breasts. "You're going to have to prove it to me."

Kar'four sighed, his brow wrinkling as he pulled Sam into his side and tilted her chin upward with his fist. "When are you going to learn to trust us?"

"That's okay," Deuce told his brother, "there's a limo waiting downstairs." He threw a glance around the crowded room, raising his voice to be heard over the booming conversation and laughter. "Are you guys ready to ride?"

* * * * *

Fighting their way across town through the busy New Las Vegas traffic, it was an hour before the stretch Hummer pulled up to a pretty ranch-style home in a clean neighborhood. A young man had just finished mowing the lawn. When he saw the Hummer emptying onto the road in front of his home, he rubbed his palms into his jeans and loped across the yard to meet his guests.

The cowboy stuck out his hand and Deuce grasped it. He shook Four's hand next, bobbing his head at the rest of the brothers and winking for the three ladies. "Thanks fer the house, mates."

"All part of the *deal*," Deuce told him, emphasizing the last word sternly. "Is Sydney's sister inside?"

"That's right," the cowboy answered, glancing back at the house as he dragged his fingers through his blond hair. The sun glinted bright against a piece of jewelry on his hand.

"What's that on your finger?" Four choked out in surprise.

"This?" The cowboy twisted the gold band on his ring finger. "Oh...you know..." He scratched the back of his head while he squinted at Kar'four. "Well, you wanted me to make an honest woman out of her. I thought the wedding was a good place to start."

A slow grin spread across Four's hard mouth.

"You shoulda been there!" the newlywed enthused. "I ordered the thirty-minute special. There was rose petals and music and witnesses and everything! Wedding cake and champagne! Pictures! They threw in the personalized champagne glasses, free! Etched with our names entwined together. You don't get much more fucking romantic than that."

Kar'four tried to tamp down the edges of his smile. "Well I'm glad to hear the rehabilitation is going well but what about...the punishment? That *was* part of the agreement."

The cowboy glanced at the watch on his wrist. "Right. I was just going in to give her her spanking when you guys pulled up."

"Spanking?" Sam sputtered out. She clapped a hand over her mouth before anyone could see she wasn't properly horrified. Unfortunately, she couldn't hide the glee that twinkled in her eyes. She caught Jerri's expression and was somewhat mollified to find her best friend hiding a rebellious grin of her own. But no one noticed because at that moment a slender figure appeared on the other side of the neat little home's screen door. Sydney's sister tugged at the hem of a short red camisole that barely covered her ass. "Cowboy," she called out in a plaintive voice, "Isn't it time for my spanking?"

The young blond turned his head. "I'll be right there, love." He grinned at his guests as he pushed his shoulders back and sighed. His eyes sparkled. "Sorry, mates. Duty calls."

"Right," Deuce told him understandingly. "It's a dirty job but somebody has to do it."

"A cowboy's work is never done," Four threw in, forcing a sympathetic look onto his face.

With a boyish grin lighting his features, the cowboy backed away then turned and jogged toward the door of his new home.

Sixpack crossed his arms over his chest. "Are we done here?" he asked in a bored drawl.

Deuce arched an eyebrow at Sam and Jerri who shared a brief look. "We're done here," they answered together.

"Good," Sixpack said, throwing his arm around Tré's shoulders and reaching for the Hummer's door handle. "Because there's a whole world of women out there...and we have a lot of catching up to do."

Also by Madison Hayes

ಬಿ

About the Author

⍥

Employed as an engineer, I've worked in an underground mine that went up—inside a mountain. I've swung over the Ohio River in a tiny cage suspended from a crane in the middle of an electrical storm. I've hung over the Hudson River at midnight in an aluminum boat suspended from a floating barge at the height of a blizzard, while snowplows on the bridge overhead rained slush and salt down on my shoulders. You can't do this sort of work without developing a sense of humor and a taste for adventure.

A relative newcomer to the publishing industry, I read my first romance five years ago and decided to try my hand at writing. Both my reading and writing habits are subject to mood and I usually have several stories going at once. When I need a really good idea for a story, I clean toilets. Now there's an activity that engenders escapism.

I was surveying when I met my husband. He was my 'rod man'. While I was trying to get my crosshairs on his stadia rod, he dropped his pants and mooned me. Next thing I know, I've got the backside of paradise in my viewfinder. So I grabbed the walkie-talkie. "That's real nice," I told him, "but would you please turn around? I'd rather see the other side."

It was love at first sight.

Also by Rhyannon Byrd

ഗ

eBooks:
A Little Less Conversation
Against the Wall
Alpha Romeos *(with Madison Hayes)*
Half Wild *(with Madison Hayes)*
Horn of the Unicorn
Magick Men: A Bite of Magick
Magick Men: A Shot of Magick
Second to None
Sexy Sweet: Triple Play
Waiting For It

Print Books:
Against the Wall
Alpha Romeos *(with Madison Hayes)*
Down and Dirty *(anthology)*
Hot Chances *(anthology)*
Magick Men: A Bite of Magick
More Than Magick *(anthology)*
Sexy Sweet: Triple Play
Waiting For It

About the Author

ℛℴ

Rhyannon Byrd is the wife of a Brit, mother of two amazing children, and maid to a precocious beagle named Misha. A longtime fan of romance, she finally felt at home when she read her first Romantica novel. Her love of this spicy, ever-changing genre has become an unquenchable passion—the hotter they are, the better she enjoys them!

Writing for Ellora's Cave is a dream come true for Rhyannon. Now her days (and let's face it, most nights) are spent giving life to the stories and characters running wild in her head. Whether she's writing contemporaries, paranormals...or even futuristics, there's always sure to be a strong Alpha hero featured as well as a fascinating woman to capture his heart, keeping all that wicked wildness for her own!

Rhyannon loves to hear from readers.

The authors welcome comments from readers. You can find their websites and email addresses on their author bio pages at www.ellorascave.com.

Tell Us What You Think

We appreciate hearing reader opinions about our books. You can email us at Comments@EllorasCave.com.

Why an electronic book?

We live in the Information Age—an exciting time in the history of human civilization, in which technology rules supreme and continues to progress in leaps and bounds every minute of every day. For a multitude of reasons, more and more avid literary fans are opting to purchase e-books instead of paper books. The question from those not yet initiated into the world of electronic reading is simply: *Why?*

1. ***Price.*** An electronic title at Ellora's Cave Publishing and Cerridwen Press runs anywhere from 40% to 75% less than the cover price of the exact same title in paperback format. Why? Basic mathematics and cost. It is less expensive to publish an e-book (no paper and printing, no warehousing and shipping) than it is to publish a paperback, so the savings are passed along to the consumer.

2. ***Space.*** Running out of room in your house for your books? That is one worry you will never have with electronic books. For a low one-time cost, you can purchase a handheld device specifically designed for e-reading. Many e-readers have large, convenient screens for viewing. Better yet, hundreds of titles can be stored within your new library—on a single microchip. There are a variety of e-readers from different manufacturers. You can also read e-books on your PC or laptop computer. (Please note that Ellora's Cave does not endorse any specific brands.

You can check our websites at www.ellorascave.com or www.cerridwenpress.com for information we make available to new consumers.)

3. *Mobility.* Because your new e-library consists of only a microchip within a small, easily transportable e-reader, your entire cache of books can be taken with you wherever you go.

4. **Personal Viewing Preferences.** Are the words you are currently reading too small? Too large? Too… ANNOYING? Paperback books cannot be modified according to personal preferences, but e-books can.

5. *Instant Gratification.* Is it the middle of the night and all the bookstores near you are closed? Are you tired of waiting days, sometimes weeks, for bookstores to ship the novels you bought? Ellora's Cave Publishing sells instantaneous downloads twenty-four hours a day, seven days a week, every day of the year. Our webstore is never closed. Our e-book delivery system is 100% automated, meaning your order is filled as soon as you pay for it.

Those are a few of the top reasons why electronic books are replacing paperbacks for many avid readers.

As always, Ellora's Cave and Cerridwen Press welcome your questions and comments. We invite you to email us at Comments@ellorascave.com or write to us directly at Ellora's Cave Publishing Inc., 1056 Home Avenue, Akron, OH 44310-3502.

COMING TO A BOOKSTORE NEAR YOU!

ELLORA'S CAVE

Bestselling Authors Tour

UPDATES AVAILABLE AT

WWW.ELLORASCAVE.COM

ELLORA'S CAVE
Romanticon

Annual convention
for women who
refuse to behave

Discover for yourself why readers can't get enough
of the multiple award-winning publisher
Ellora's Cave.

Whether you prefer e-books or paperbacks,

be sure to visit EC on the web at
www.ellorascave.com

for an erotic reading experience that will leave you
breathless.

3282236R00110

Printed in Great Britain
by Amazon.co.uk, Ltd.,
Marston Gate.